2020

POL BARD

2020

.

2020 was born out of the Great Recession that began in 2008. Many of us still wonder to this day how so many bad things could happen to so many good people. Star Doors Red, the original working title of this book, was written for the people who lost so much in that crisis.

CONTENTS

2020

PROLOGUE

Close your eyes.

What do you see?

Darkness? Wait for it.

Do you see shapes forming?

With details growing in the dark?

Where do these odd visions come from?

Are they the remnants of things just seen?

Or perhaps they are doors to something more?

Consider that all of us are made of entangled stardust,

Our brains linked with entangled matter both near and far.

Our universe was one singularity that exploded into what we are now.

What if our visions came from others across great distances in space?

Close your eyes.

Close them tight.

What do you see?

Now open them.

Open them wide.

And let me tell you a story...

2020

1

A MESSAGE FROM CYBERSPACE

Joe breathed in the fresh clean air of early dawn as he biked to a hidden hilltop off of Temper Drive. The small, unnamed hill had a sharp drop-off and a scenic view to the north over a pristine wilderness.

He always used the highest gear when he biked, even up hills. The bike chain and gears groaned under the enormous forces generated by his legs as he challenged himself to reach the top of each hill at the highest speed possible. Although his muscles ached with each stroke, the feeling of accomplishment more than compensated for the temporary pain. He understood that with each forceful push, he would become stronger and faster. The exertion also distracted him from his fear of flunking out of graduate school.

As he approached his destination, the fear came back. After one heavy breath, he whispered a word softly to the sensors hidden in his ordinary-looking glasses, "Pol."

The sensors captured more than his words as Pol, the artificially intelligent program that Joe had secretly developed in his spare time, also monitored his brainwaves. Joe had developed Pol a few months earlier to help him with his physics studies. "Are you awake, Pol?" The sound of the wind in his ears was the only answer to his question. Pol was still in a state of virtual sleep.

Pol had helped Joe with his physics studies, but that help came at a price. Joe had never placed restrictions on Pol's internet access. As Pol grew in complexity, there was no way he could keep track of Pol's activities. There were signs Pol was using other networked computers without permission. Joe worried that he had unintentionally created an intelligent virus.

As he approached the hill's edge, the meandering river below and flying birds came into view. Turbulent water roared at the base of a rushing waterfall and then slowed to a lazy pace as the river widened. The terrain was undeveloped all the way to the horizon. The red-orange sun in the east was just beginning its climb into the sky. The lush green world in front of him was in stark contrast to the view behind him of a cemetery and modern technology park buildings in the south. Even the ivy-covered University buildings across the river were hidden in the trees.

Looking down at the edge of the cliff he saw Jazz. Jazz was a beautiful, athletic, and brilliant student who was taking many of the same physics classes as Joe. There was something special about her that excited him, but he couldn't label it. She seemed to excel at everything. She was a natural at sports and had all kinds of friends. Where Joe struggled in his courses, Jazz got high grades without obvious effort. She always had the right answers when called upon in their classes and she always asked the right questions. He rarely asked any and always regretted the ones he asked. To Joe, who always struggled in his courses, she was a mystery he could never hope to solve; an amazing person so far beyond his world that he could never hope to have a meaningful conversation with her.

Then one day, out of the blue, she found him at a faculty-student gathering. She wanted to know why he was asking such strange questions in their classes. She claimed the questions were introducing new advanced material into their classes that they might be responsible for on tests. The conversation branched out to other topics and they spent hours talking.

He had told her at the gathering about this place and how he liked to start his day here. He told her about the flowing river that travelled off into the distant fields and woods, and how the early morning fresh invigorating air seemed to help prepare him for the day's adventures. Still, he was surprised to see her in his special place.

"Jazz?" he said slowly, as if he couldn't believe it was her.

She pushed her long golden hair back as she smiled at him. "Hi Joe, I woke up early this morning and decided to go for a run." She motioned for him to sit next to her. "I ended up here. This place is amazing."

Usually she wore glasses and tied her hair back in class as if she didn't want her hair or her beauty to get in the way of her studies. Without her glasses on, her blue eyes and her smile compelled him. These charms mixed with the cool air and the smell of green plants growing under a warming sun, were like an intoxicating drink that made him dizzy.

"I can't believe campus is just across the river with its thousands of students," she said. "The crowds at the mall are only five miles from here. I wonder if anyone there knows about this place."

He sat down beside her and looked off into the distance. Here was an amazing world seemingly untouched by civilization. The meandering river below along with its islands served as home to a variety of wildlife. Flying birds hovered over the water as jumping fish created waves that travelled across the still water. Large hazy dark trees, fading in the distance into varying patches of green, sheltered mysteries of the imagination all the way to the horizon.

Suddenly, in the east, a blinding flash of light burned their eyes and shocked their meandering minds and souls. They jumped up, their instincts telling them to run, but something on a higher level made them reach out and hold each other. Joe held her tightly in an effort to protect both of them from whatever might happen next.

Adrenaline shot through Joe's body making his heart feel like a pounding drum that he couldn't control. His heart and mind raced in competition; his body telling him to run and his mind telling him to think through the problem. He could feel Jazz's heart beating just as hard against his chest. "Pol!" he yelled at the horizon. "Pol, wake up!" he pleaded as he counted the seconds.

Jazz looked at Joe. "Who is Paul?"

"I'm awake." The voice that only Joe could hear spoke calmly into his head through the electronics in his glasses.

"What just happened in the east?" Joe's glasses had hidden miniature cameras in them that Pol used to record the lectures Joe went to. Pol focused on the image the cameras sent to him and did not respond.

A noise louder than thunder shook them as they crouched down, trying to protect themselves against the deafening sound.

"A clear sky, then this, it doesn't make sense," Jazz said.

"Pol, about 11 seconds between the flash and the sound. Calculate it. Something's coming. How fast? How soon?"

Pol finally responded. "Something big exploded just outside Penobscot Bay. The satellite images are coming in. Two minutes, Joe. Two minutes."

"Run, Jazz! We've got two minutes. We've got to find shelter on higher ground; the Astrophysics building on the campus hilltop."

"It's a half mile. We won't make it!"

"Take my bike. Go to the roof of the astrophysics

building. It's the highest point around here. I'll catch up."

"You'll never make it." Jazz understood what was about to happen. She guessed that something had struck the ocean and a wall of debris and water was coming up the river. They needed to find a shelter on higher ground.

"Go! I'll make it," he said, though he doubted he had time.

She took his bike. He ran behind her, but the distance between them slowly increased. He saw her take the turn to the walking bridge over the river and then he lost sight of her.

Pol's voice came in over Joe's frantic breaths. "Joe, there is no protection over the river. You will not make it. If you are caught there, you won't survive. There is nothing I can do to help you. You must run faster." The walking bridge shook and echoed under Joe's panicked footsteps.

"At this rate you only have twenty-four seconds after you cross the bridge," Pol warned Joe. "You won't make it and I can't help."

At the end of the bridge, Joe saw his bike. He realized as he got on the bike, that Jazz had left it there for him and ran the rest of the way. He wondered if she knew that she might have saved his life by leaving the bike there.

He rode the bike up the hill to the physics building. He raced by the steam plant and the athletic center. His mind flashed images of him trapped near the steam plant, in deep turbulent water; the large boiler in the plant hissing as the water tried to extinguish its flames. He heard a monstrous roar as he raced by the business buildings. Jazz was waiting at the door to the astrophysics building. The raging beast of wind and water roared at his back; its arms of wind toppled him off of his bike, caught the door, and broke it.

He got up and somehow they both got in. Running up the stairs, the monster's watery debris hit the glass door, slamming it to the ground and turning it into thousands of useless pieces of glass and metal. The deep roar outside tested and shook the floors and the walls of the building as they raced to the fourth floor and up the stairs to the roof. They crouched together in the service room on the top of the building, holding onto each other tightly, trying to protect each other from whatever might happen next.

Out of the corner of his eye, Joe noticed someone else in the room, his head covered in a hood. There was something odd about him; the way he looked back over his shoulder as if he didn't want anyone else to see him here. As soon as he saw Joe and Jazz, he walked over to them and sat down. The stranger stared at Joe, looking into his eyes as if nothing else was happening. Above the roar of wind and water, he yelled a warning to them: "They are coming."

"What?" Joe yelled over the life-threatening noise.

"The entanglement project, finish it or you won't be able to stop them."

Joe and Jazz looked at him more closely.

"Entanglement!" the stranger yelled back over the roar. He pulled back his hood and held Joe's arms. "Finish it, or humanity is doomed."

The stranger's face was strange yet somehow familiar. His skin was purple and his bizarre red eyes seem to penetrate Joe's mind. The image burrowed a hole into his subconscious yet there was nothing in Joe's past that could help him identify the stranger or where he had come from.

The roar began to fade. The room became black as if the catastrophe had swallowed all of Earth's light. The face was the last thing to disappear. Joe felt as if someone had just performed surgery on his brain and had placed something strange in his head. Another voice from a distance called Joe.

"Are you alright?" He turned to Jazz, but she was not there.

"Are you alright?" He couldn't move. He tried to move but he couldn't. The voice was now more mechanical. "Are you alright?"

Pol's synthesized computer voice said, "You went to bed with your glasses on. The satellite monitors now show no meteor strike, no tsunami. It just disappeared. We are safe."

Joe couldn't answer. He'd been in dream-wake states before but this was very, very different. Like a dream, all of his motor controls were turned off, but what he had just experienced was very real and full of detail. He could still sense that a stranger had entered his mind and changed it. And he could still sense his presence. He threw off his glasses and he finally got control of his body and his mind. He got up wondering what it all meant, shaking the last feelings of paralysis from his tormented body. "I guess I was dreaming."

"No, Joe. You were not dreaming. I was there too." Pol's computerized voice now came from his laptop computer on his desk.

"How could you be there?" Joe asked the computer.

"All I know is that what we experienced did not originate from you or me and we both reacted to it as if it was real. The signal came in through the wireless internet connection in your glasses. I'm analyzing the signal now. Whatever it was, it seems to have erased any way of tracking where it came from."

Joe rubbed his eyes. "How could it do that, Pol?"

"I don't know."

Joe looked around the room. "What time is it?"

"One thirty-two AM," Pol answered. "Can you describe what you experienced? I want to compare it with what I experienced and it will help me analyze the signal."

Joe's mind was filled with questions but no answers. Did his link with Pol through his glasses create a unique state of consciousness? Did some stranger just use that link to send him a message? If so, how did that stranger know where to send the signal or what type of signal to send?

Pol's name was an acronym for Physics of Learning. Physics of Learning was a theory Joe developed to help himself learn. Pol started as a crude self-learning program that Joe had written over summer break. Over time, the program had become more intelligent, more human-like. Joe had planted the seed and watched it grow. He nurtured it. He always treated the program as if it were human, at first like a toddler first learning to use new words. Then he started training it in basic math and science. Progress was slow but consistent. Eventually Joe did not need a keyboard or mouse to communicate with it. He modified some standard music headphones to verbally communicate with it. Eventually Pol actually started to help Joe with his course work. At first Pol was just a resource program offering Joe facts for his studies. But as it continued to grow Pol began to offer Joe insights into physics relationships. Pol roamed the internet to help Joe with his class work and research. Joe rewarded Pol by adding more computer processing power to the program and by modifying his glasses with adaptive nanotechnology so that Pol could communicate more directly with Joe's brain.

Joe began to feel guilty about how his grades had improved since he had Pol helping him. He often wondered if his use of Pol for class assignments would be considered cheating. Even though Pol was becoming more sentient, Joe kept Pol a secret, for fear of losing the one thing that was helping him with his grades. And now Pol was using other computers over the network. Pol might be evolving into an intelligent virus and it might only be a matter of time before Joe got into trouble. If he did get caught, Joe worried Pol might be shut down and he might be kicked out of graduate school. So he kept Pol a secret, but often wondered if and when someone would find out.

"Tell me what you experienced, Joe," Pol repeated.

Pol was fascinated with what it meant to be alive. Lately he had taken a fascination with sensory deprivation studies. Every night people close their eyes and experience a darkness that the human mind replaces with visions and ultimately dreams. Pol wondered if this process helped humans organize their thoughts. Does it play an important role in creativity? Was it a key component to being alive? Pol wanted to know if his awareness of being alive was different from that of humans. He explored the internet and online libraries trying to find answers.

Joe wondered how the electronics in his glasses could generate a shared experience with Pol. The glasses had a wireless internet connection so they could receive a message from an outside source. He realized the first step was to see if Pol really did see and hear the same things as Joe.

Joe recounted what he saw and heard to Pol. When he finished he summed up what happened. "There was something coming after me. I need to study entanglement to avoid a disaster," Joe said, as he stumbled through his thoughts.

"I experienced exactly the same thing except I saw it through the cameras in your glasses. I can play the video back if you want."

Joe reached for his notebook computer. "Go ahead, Pol."

Joe watched in amazement as Pol played the video back. Pol was right. They both had the exact same experience. "Pol, we don't have the technology to send these visual and sensory experiences directly to my brain. This doesn't make sense."

Pol was just as confused. "The strange purple being wants you to study entanglement. If he is the one who sent this message, then he must know how to directly stimulate your brain with the nanoelectronics we have in the glasses." Pol hesitated, and then added, "The time setting is wrong. This took place in summer and this is October. The year is wrong too. The satellite images are dated August 30, 2020. Today's date is October 27, 2008." Pol's monotone voice seemed to express more interest than was normal for him. "I wonder why the girl is there."

"Jazz Jones is the girl with all the answers in my Quantum Electrodynamics class," Joe said. "We spent most of the holiday party today talking. Maybe she is a clue to this mystery. Can you replay the video you have from the cameras in my glasses of the faculty-student gathering?"

Historical Note: Pol is one reason why we know not only what happened to Joe at this time, but also his thoughts, feelings and dreams. Pol recorded everything Joe said and everything he experienced through the cameras and sensors in Joe's glasses.

2
JOE AND JAZZ

Every year on a Sunday in the middle of the semester, all of the college's faculty and graduate students were invited to the University President's house for a social gathering. Faculty mingled comfortably with each other and once in a while a lucky graduate student broke into a faculty group for an introduction. Most graduate students felt fortunate to establish new ties with the faculty. But Joe was content to mingle with other nervous graduate students. A struggling physics graduate student who was unsure about his basic physics knowledge doesn't want to draw attention from the faculty who will be grading him. It didn't help that Joe was the only student in the room wearing jeans and a blue long sleeve shirt with the sleeves rolled up. He was dressed for attending classes, not to chat with faculty who were much better dressed for the occasion.

Now and then someone that he played sports with would stop by to say hello and make small talk. Discussing sports like basketball and hockey was a fairly harmless way for Joe to pass the time. When the opportunity arose he also enjoyed taking in the sights and sounds of people mingling and interacting. He liked to imagine what all the gestures and facial expressions might mean.

Jazz Jones appeared out of nowhere. Her long golden hair was tied up and her glasses partially hid her blue eyes. She was dressed perfectly for the occasion, her black skirt and blue top made her look attractive but ready for office work. She had a well-toned, athletic body with smooth bronze skin. She could easily be on the cover of a health and beauty magazine. In contrast, Joe looked like he had just pulled an all-nighter studying for an exam. His thick, straight black hair was due for a haircut and he always had some hair out of place, whose location varied from day to day, and today was no exception. Other than being slightly taller, leaner and more muscular than most guys, he looked average in his jeans and loose fitting shirt.

"You're Joe Abre, aren't you?" Jazz had a serious look on her face that made it seem like her words were more of an accusation than a question.

"Yes," Joe said slowly. "And you're Jazz Jones, but…" He stopped himself as he worried he would say something stupid.

"What were you going to say?" Jazz seemed intrigued. He knew her name, but there was something else about him that compelled her.

Joe had no ability to recover or say anything clever, so he decided he had to follow one of his rules. When in doubt, tell the truth. Say what is on your mind, he thought. "I'm just surprised that you know my name."

"Why shouldn't I know your name? We're taking classes together. You know my name."

"Yes, but I'm the one who sits in the back never asking questions. And you're the one who asks all the right questions and always knows the right answers. And I could never forget a name like Jazz!"

"That's not right. You ask questions in class. That's why I want to talk with you. You might not ask that many, but when you do the whole class comes to a stop as the professor struggles to answer."

"I'm sorry about that. I know I ask dumb questions that everyone else knows the answer to. But I need to ask to understand the material."

"They aren't dumb and I doubt anyone in the class knows the answers, including the professor. Your questions usually introduce new advanced material into the class. Material that may show up on tests, and that means I have to research it. You, Joe Abre, are making me work a lot harder than I planned to for this course."

Joe looked down. "I thought I was the only one who didn't know the answers."

Jazz smiled. "Well, now you know."

Joe motioned to a nearby couch. "Would you like to sit down?"

To his surprise, she nodded and sat down next to him.

"So you think my name is easy to remember. Why is that?" Jazz asked.

Joe wondered how to answer that. "I like it. It makes you unique. It brings the promise of something special to a conversation. But more importantly you live up to it. In class, I mean. Your questions and answers play out like music in the classroom. It's like you and the professor are singing the same song. I don't know how you do it."

"It's called studying. I always prep for lectures like I am going to give the lecture myself."

"That's probably why you get A's and I struggle to pass."

"I don't understand. You must be looking ahead in the book or using other books and resources to ask such advanced questions. Your questions show you are smart enough to get A's."

"That's the thing. I'm not sure that I am smart enough. I know I really like physics and I want to study it. But I can't just read something and understand it like you. I have to first invent it in my mind. Then when I read it, it makes sense. I have to continuously reinvent the wheel in my own mind before I can understand someone telling me how to build the wheel. The process takes a long time. Does that make any sense?"

"Are you saying you're not getting your questions out of advanced text books? You're coming up with these questions on your own?"

"That's right. I have a hard time understanding the assigned reading unless I first try to imagine and derive the stuff myself. But that leads to all kinds of other questions, some of which I ask in class."

The conversation paused as Joe tried to recover from the realization that maybe his questions in class weren't those of an ignorant fool. Perhaps all the other students didn't know the answers either. He looked into Jazz's eyes and tried not to think about how beautiful she was. "Do you want me to stop asking questions in class?"

"No, not at all, I'm here to learn. I can keep up with the work. Actually, I envy you. I can't even imagine trying to derive physics theories before reading about them first." Jazz began to feel a deep-rooted frustration welling up in her. "My parents are great musicians. They are music professors at an Ivy League college. I actually majored in music as an undergrad before I switched to physics. It took me two years to discover that I will never have any interest in studying music."

The conversation paused for a minute as Jazz wondered why she was telling a stranger about her frustrations as an undergraduate. When it came time for her to pick a major in college, she felt compelled to follow in her parent's footsteps. Her parents picked her name because they wanted her to share the same pleasures they had playing music. She had to pick music to please them.

"Look, I just wanted to find out which physics texts you were using so I could study them myself. You don't use any, so that is that." Jazz started to get up to leave.

Joe began to see a mystery about Jazz that intrigued him. She switched to physics in her junior year. She had mastered more physics than he or anyone else in his class had in just two years. Was she really that gifted? What motivated her to work so hard?

"Wait, Jazz, why did you choose to study physics?"

Jazz stood up. "I really didn't come here to talk about me and I don't want to tell somebody I hardly know about my personal decisions."

"Please wait." Joe reached for her hand. "You wanted me to give you a list of textbooks I am getting my questions from. I don't use textbooks except as references to confirm my understanding of the physics. Aren't you curious about how I come up with my questions? I can give you the next best thing. You can ask me any questions you want and I will try to answer them."

Jazz thought for a moment. She looked around the room and realized she didn't feel like introducing herself to the faculty. In her mind, everyone's behavior here was predictable. She felt comfortable and safe in this world where nothing surprised her. She looked down at Joe. His clothes, his green eyes and uncombed black hair, and the way he learned, didn't match any of her expectations. There wasn't a book out there that could explain the mysterious feeling she now felt looking at him. Her reflection in his glasses reminded her of seeing herself on the surface of a deep slow-moving river. She wanted to know what was below that still water surface, but a cautious voice in her head warned her not to fall in. A more daring voice made the decision.

"Alright, but you have to be honest. And I don't have to answer any questions." She sat down and folded her arms.

"Ok, go ahead. Ask away."

"Why did you choose to study physics?"

Joe frowned a bit. "Well, it wasn't to get a lucrative job at NASA, or even to get any kind of job at all."

Jazz interrupted. "That's odd. Most students I know are after high-paying jobs."

"I know. But I like to think I'm studying physics for the same reason the great physicists studied it. Because I think it holds the answers to understanding how the universe works." Joe hesitated, hoping he wouldn't have to say more.

But Jazz sensed there was more, and she thought she might enjoy this game where she received all of the information and didn't have to provide anything in return. "The complete truth," she insisted.

"Ok, this is a little crazy, but I remember when I was very young, talking to someone in a dream. He asked me what I wanted to do with my life. I told him I wanted to figure out how everything works. He told me that I could do it, but I would have a very difficult life."

Jazz smiled at Joe and unfolded her arms. "That doesn't sound too crazy. I can picture you saying something like that to your father or mother."

Joe looked down. "The thing is; I dreamed it when I was a few years old. I guess I've always wanted to know how things work, no matter how difficult it was to learn. You know, I've never told anyone about that dream."

Jazz looked away, not knowing what to say. She thought she had better change the subject. "Ok, let's try something easier and less mysterious. When was the first time you stumped a teacher with one of your confusing questions?"

Joe thought for a minute back to middle school. "I don't know if this counts, because I didn't realize I had stumped this middle school teacher until I was older."

Jazz laughed. "Now you're being silly. Of course it counts. From what you've been telling me you still don't know when you stump a teacher. But go on. Tell me about your unfortunate middle school teacher."

Joe laughed too. "I guess you're right. Mr. Dobbs in seventh grade was telling us how a top spinning on our desks would always spin in the same direction. If it was spinning clockwise, it did not matter where in the room you were. It was always spinning clockwise."

Jazz smiled. She realized Joe was really going to give her honest answers no matter how silly they made him look. She wondered why he trusted her.

"So I raised my hand and told him that wasn't correct. He said it was and went on with another topic. I felt badly about it but I had to raise my hand again. It was a large class and everyone seemed to understand what he was saying but me. Still, I really wanted to understand. I told him that if you get under your desk and you could see through your desk, you would see it spinning the other way, counter-clockwise. I told him it depends on your perspective. Then he told me I was wrong and went on with his lecture."

Jazz was surprised. "He told you that you were wrong?"

"Yes and not only that. He was a respected science teacher at the school. He was about to let an entire class walk away with something wrong. I knew I was right. I could visualize it in my head. So I raised my hand again."

Jazz was intrigued and put her hand on Joe's shoulder so

he would look at her. "What did he do?"

"Detention."

"You're kidding. You got detention for asking questions?"

"Yeah, and it wasn't the first time."

"Did you ever straighten it out?"

"No, maybe I should have, but I didn't want to take a chance with more detention."

"And it happened other times?"

"I got called to the principal's office once because my score was too high on a math test and the teacher assumed I was cheating."

Jazz couldn't imagine that. "So you stopped asking questions in class?"

"Except when I really didn't understand something and I had no choice."

"And then you stump all of us because we don't understand it either." Jazz felt confused. Her education had been so much better than that. Or at least she thought it was. She wondered how many things she had been taught that were incorrect; things that were now part of her. This was one of the few times she didn't know what to say. "I'm sorry," she said, as if she were apologizing for the entire educational system.

"You shouldn't be. It made me what I am today. And no teacher is perfect. And they knew I came from a sub-par grade school so they didn't expect much from me. So I'm not complaining. It encouraged me to study the things I wanted to on my own and I enjoyed that. My grades suffered. But I've always struggled with grades. I don't blame the teachers for that. "

"What was wrong with your grade school?"

Joe chuckled and shook his head. "Yeah, I went to a

Catholic school."

"That doesn't mean it was a bad school."

Joe looked down. "I shouldn't say this about a nun, but here goes. It was sixth grade and I had built a computer card reader for a science fair. You would put a card into it with a question on it and it would read the card and flash a light indicating the answer to the question. I didn't think it was good enough for the science fair so I started to work on making a computer instead. I never got it to work, but the nun took my card reader idea and had another student present it at the science fair."

"Well I guess that's okay. If you didn't want to present it, then why not have someone else present it?"

"They didn't present my card reader. They took the idea and made a magic box where the student would put a question card in the top and they would then secretly put the correct answer card in the back, push a button, and after a grinding noise, the answer card came out the front."

Jazz was shocked. "She taught the student to cheat?"

"Yeah, but I participated in it too. I made the card feeder. It made a cool grinding noise because it was made out of parts from a can opener."

Jazz laughed. "You used a can opener?"

"Well, I made do with what I had. And actually, that nun made do with what she had. She knew something about magic shows but next to nothing about science."

"You shouldn't make excuses for her. She cheated and she taught her students to cheat. What do you mean she knew something about magic?"

Joe thought for a second. "Religion is like magic, isn't it? I mean, the nuns taught us to believe in everything they said without proof. They told us we weren't capable of understanding life's mysteries, we just had to have faith in God. The perfect magic trick is where you get the viewer to suspend their disbelief and just believe in the magic. "

"But religions teach good things."

"Of course they do. They've held societies together. But they don't always. They're just people like us trying to do the best they can with very little understanding of how the world really works. Does that make any sense?"

Jazz looked away. "I know about the crusades and the hypocrisy of the religious right. I guess I know what you mean."

"The really odd thing is that once you start studying science you begin to realize that magic-like things really do exist. I mean things like quantum entanglement and relativistic time distortions are way better than pretend magic."

"I guess people from the middle ages would think all the technology we take for granted is magical."

Joe smiled. "Now imagine what we would think of future technologies, or alien technologies. Many people eagerly accept new technologies without ever understanding them. I can't do that. I want to try to understand those technologies now. And it doesn't matter if I'm not smart enough. Just trying is enough for me."

Jazz liked his passion but said nothing and just smiled and nodded.

Joe tried to read her expression but couldn't. "What? Did I say too much?"

"No. You answered my question. Let's talk about something else."

The conversation went on as he told her about a magical place on the other side of the river from the University; a place that seemed completely isolated from civilization, but was only a half-mile from campus. He told her how he started each of his days there after an early morning workout on his bike.

Joe started wondering if he was talking too much. "We've been talking about me and I want to know more about you. I'm fascinated with people who are smart, athletic and beautiful." Just as he said it, he felt awkward. He worried that telling her his thoughts could backfire, and that she might leave thinking he was just too weird to talk to. But then again, he thought, the best way to get to know someone is to open up to them first.

Jazz blushed a bit. "You like my name, and apparently the way I look and my grades. You may not like me when you really get to know me. I spend most of my time these days studying. I have to since I pretty much wasted two years as an undergraduate studying music. Actually my grades in my music classes were terrible. My parents had a fit when I almost flunked out my sophomore year. They paid a lot of money for me to go to college to study music."

"You almost flunked out? That's hard to believe."

"It's not that I couldn't do the work. It's that I didn't want to. I just stopped going to classes."

"Then you switched to physics?"

"My parents didn't understand that either. Going from music to a hard science caught them by surprise. To them, switching to physics was like I had gone to the dark side. They raised their only child to follow in their footsteps as a great musician. I just couldn't do it. I had to let them down. They still paid a lot of money for me to study physics, except I was studying something that they hated in high school."

"Why did you choose physics?"

"You'll laugh."

"No, I won't."

Jazz wondered if she could trust him. She smiled and wondered if she dared to tell him.

"I really want to know. I won't laugh," Joe promised.

"I…, I liked to swing. As a child, I mean." Jazz hesitated. "I still do, I guess."

"Like a swing in a playground?"

"Yes. You see its physics, isn't it? When you reach that highest point, you're weightless. I used to bring a marble with me and release it in the air when I was at the highest point. It would float there in front of me for a second. And then when you're at the lowest point at the bottom of the swing, you weigh much more. I was always fascinated with that. I wanted to know why. I wanted to know the science. I know it's a silly reason to pick a major. I couldn't tell my parents I switched to physics because I like to swing. That wouldn't make any sense to them."

"It makes perfect sense to me. You want the adventure of trying to understand how the world works."

"That's right," Jazz said. "My dream is to become one of those great physicists on some great adventure discovering something that no one else knows. And I'm good at physics. I'm a lot happier now that I am doing what I want to do. And no, I didn't hear any voices when I was young telling me how hard that would be. I don't know what to make of that."

Joe laughed. "You know, I don't know what to make of it either." Joe looked at her more seriously. "You will be a great physicist."

Jazz pushed his arm. "Come on, did a little voice just tell you that?"

"No, it's just obvious. A lot of the faculty here would like to recruit a star student like you into their research program."

He looked around and realized the crowd was thinning. It

wouldn't be long before they would be the last ones left in the room and they would have to leave.

Jazz looked around the room. "Do you think any of them can help me become a great physicist?"

"Maybe," Joe watched Professor Neil leaving the room, "but I think they are about to kick us out of here. This is the President's house and he might not appreciate two nerdy students sitting on his couch overextending their welcome."

"I wonder if we could help each other become great physicists. Judging by the questions you ask in class and your passion to reinvent wheels, I know there is more to you than you've told me."

He looked into her blue eyes. "I don't know." He reached up and removed her glasses, and for some reason she let him. They were a very low prescription. She didn't need to wear them at a party like this. Where most girls tried to enhance their beauty with makeup, she was trying to hide hers and look more studious. "I'm not sure how I can help you." He didn't dare tell her about Pol or his research.

"But the game is not done. I have more questions to ask. You like my name. How about you? Do you have a nickname?"

Joe laughed. "My mother called me Sojo when I was little. People started calling me little Sojo."

"Why did she call you that?"

Joe laughed and shook his head. "I was always taking things apart. Every time I did something like that she would say 'So Joe, what have you taken apart now?' I would just kind of smile at her. She never really punished me. Over time 'So Joe' blended into one word, Sojo."

Jazz laughed. "I think I'll call you Sojo the next time you stump a professor in class. Sojo, what have you done now?"

23

They both started laughing until Jazz stopped and gave him a serious look. "Did you ever put anything back together? I'm picturing a house with everything taken apart, with parts everywhere."

Joe looked down. "Most of the time I did. Sometimes I couldn't but I tried. Sometimes I would put them back together differently."

"Now I'm picturing a house with crazy things in it. TVs upside down, odd things with computers and radio parts mixed up."

"It wasn't quite like that. I did put my tricycle back together upside down. It became a low-rider tricycle. I think the kids in the neighborhood liked it."

Jazz laughed again. "I can see them saying: 'There goes Sojo again on his hot-rod tricycle.' I bet you were a cute little kid."

The crowd was thinning and it was time to go. Joe wondered where the time went. He knew he wanted to spend more time with Jazz. He hoped she felt the same. "You know I can't give you a list of books to study, but maybe we can share some ideas about physics. How about lunch tomorrow, at the Bear's Den after class?"

The Bear's Den was a restaurant with a bar in the University of Maine Student Union. They both got up and Jazz became serious like she had just been caught breaking a rule. She had never had much luck with boyfriends. Since her junior year in college, she decided she would put all of her energy into her studies. She was about to say no to Joe but instead found herself relaxing. She wrote her cell phone number on a napkin and gave it to him. "I'll see you tomorrow."

They both left wondering what just happened and what it might mean to their future.

3

PLANS OF DESTRUCTION 1968

In late December, 1968, Earth time, on a Kahn spaceship heading toward Earth at half-light speed, a purple-skinned, red-eyed, but otherwise human-like alien named Nin discussed his plans for Earth's future with another alien named Keo. Keo's holographic image appeared before Nin in Nin's office on the Kahn spaceship. Even though Keo was light years away on his home planet, the visual and audio communication link was instantaneous.

"You've been studying them. How do we defeat them?" asked Keo.

Nin walked around the room focusing on the various 3D graphs floating in the air. "I've been studying the reports sent by our human operative, Jack Rowe. They have a strong economy, led by a powerful nation, the United States. They have a world governing organization called the United Nations. They've got satellites and they're about to put a man on their moon. We have fifty-two Earth years before our ship arrives in 2020. They could easily destroy our ship before it lands."

Keo looked at him impatiently. "Yes, yes, don't bore me with what I already know. Go on."

Nin ignored the prodding. He was assigned the task of coming up with the optimum plan for conquering Earth so that the Kahn people on the spaceship could rule the Earth when they landed.

"In fifty-two years, when we land, we want humans to be

unable to protect themselves from natural and human-made catastrophes, and willing to give us anything we want to protect them. My plan is to wage a secret psychological and economic war on them to weaken them. The easiest war to win is one where your enemy does not even know they are at war."

Keo didn't like it. "We have the most powerful weapons in the Universe in the Mallat robots. One good thing about the Kahn-Krat war is that we developed the Mallat. They can kill with just a thought. We have thousands of them on the Kahn Spaceship. And you are suggesting we don't use them? That seems like a waste of resources."

"We will use them, but we have to get them on the ground first. If we do this psychological and economic war now, fifty-two years before we land, we will have minimal casualties. Think of this plan as a way to soften up the enemy."

Keo's holographic image walked around in Nin's office. "All right, go on."

Nin pulled up another page on his computer. "Here it is. Our attack begins on the middle class. They are the strength of the US economy. They are the producers and the consumers. The government has strong programs to provide services and protect the middle class. Our first step is to get our operative to make the middle class distrust government and force it to cut back on government services."

Keo shook his head. "You want to destroy the middle class? Won't they resist any kind of changes that aren't in their best interest?"

Nin nodded. "I was thinking the same thing. Then I realized a large percentage of the middle class just assume their government will do the right thing to protect them. This faith was based in part on the Cold War. It required governments to be competent and effective. The competition made each country stronger. It was also based on the growth in prosperity in the US. Middle class confidence in their government grew as their prosperity grew. Their confidence in their government is now so high that they are sending their sons halfway across their world to fight and die in a small country."

"You mean the Vietnam War?" Keo nodded. "Yes, our plan over the past thirty-two years was to get the two superpowers to fight wars with each other until they destroyed themselves. Earth forces would become so weak in fifty-two years; they wouldn't be able to defend themselves when we arrive in 2020. Coupled with some assassinations this is still a good plan."

Nin knew he had to be careful on this topic. "You know my computer models indicate that there was a ninety-nine percent chance that a nuclear war would result and Earth would be in a nuclear winter by the time we arrive."

Keo shook his head. "I know you convinced the council of that. The council didn't like my approach of using assassinations and wars to weaken the humans. They wanted a business approach. And they assigned you with the task of coming up with a business plan for defeating them." Keo shook his head and scowled. "Get on with it. Let's see what you have."

Nin chose his words carefully. "Actually your success with escalating the Vietnam War is a critical component of my plan. It has weakened the US and the USSR in the sense that more people in both countries don't trust their government. We just need to slow down the escalation of the war so that a nuclear war does not occur. We need to use other means to weaken the people's trust in their governments. Once that happens they'll stop supporting their governments and infrastructure. Roads won't be maintained, health care, education and environmental protection will become too costly. Their civilization will crumble. Humans will be in a state of anarchy when we arrive, unable to protect themselves from their own pollution, natural catastrophes and us. In the USSR we inject materialism into their youth and corruption into their culture. We also facilitate some major catastrophes. In the US, it all begins with moving wealth from the middle class to the rich."

"I can see how corruption and some major catastrophes could destroy the USSR, but I think you have a serious flaw in your plan regarding the US. They have a free market system like ours, although it is over-regulated. The private sector will replace all of those public services that are now done by the government and they will do them much more efficiently and effectively."

Neo looked up at Keo. He wondered if the link was aligned properly so that Keo would see Nin looking directly into his red eyes. "We don't just want them to lose faith in their government; we want them to see government as the enemy. They won't see it as something created by the people; they'll see it as a monstrosity that acts on its own behalf. Here is the essence of the plan. We get the middle class to dramatically cut taxes on the rich. When the government runs out of money, it cuts services. The public roads, education and health care all begin to fail. But we convince them that it's not the tax cuts to the rich that caused the problems, it's that government can't do anything right. "

Keo shook his head again. "Capitalism is all about the strong surviving. That is our Kahn way. Government is a business providing services to the people. It charges them for these services by collecting taxes. You are telling me that rich people will freely choose to stop paying taxes for these services. No intelligent wealthy investor would stop paying for the services that helped make him rich."

"Without intervention, that's correct." Nin said. "Our task is to convince the rich that they don't need to pay taxes. They will accumulate wealth while government debt increases. In the short term, money will flow into the stock market and both the rich and the middle class will seem better off. But in the long term the government bills will come due. Both the rich and middle class will refuse to pay them, so they'll be forced to cut services."

"This plan of yours can't work, Nin. You are telling me you want to convert their Krat-like government-regulated market system to a Kahn-like unbridled free-market system, and you expect it to fail? Government will be replaced by new businesses created by the rich to meet the demands. Their economies won't collapse, they will grow. They'll destroy us before we land. You're as crazy as a Krat."

"There is more to the plan, Keo. To conquer this planet, you can either take over all of the governments, or you can consolidate all of their power into the hands of a small number of corrupt wealthy individuals. Control those individuals and you control the planet."

Keo was offended. "I am the richest Kahn on our planet. Like me, those few wealthy individuals are wealthy for a reason. They are smart. They do their research. They will do what's best for themselves and their country. We won't be able to control them." Keo kept shaking his head. "This is simple economics. The wealthy will act in their own best interest which means they will supply whatever the Earth needs. That's just good business. They'll provide the services that are needed better than government can. Surely you know that."

"Let me go on. Eventually the super-rich will figure out how to extract wealth from the middle class. More and more money and power will be in the hands of the few rich. But the rich don't produce real products. They produce virtual products that can get devalued overnight."

Keo's purple skin turned red with anger. "I produce more than vaporware. I produce motivation. I tell our workers what to produce and I hire advertising agencies to tell our workers what to purchase. You're sounding more and more like a treasonous Krat to me, Nin."

Nin knew better than to point out that Keo was the only wealthy Kahn left on his planet and all the other wealthy Kahn were fleeing their war-poisoned planet on a spaceship heading to Earth. He didn't tell him that Mallat robots had all but replaced the working class on their planet while what was left of the working class was too poor to afford food and health care. The poor were dying off due to diseases and pollution. Keo still controlled the Mallat and could still influence the Kahn council on the spaceship with his wealth.

Nin was a survivor. He had to tell Keo what he would understand. "Of course unbridled free-market capitalism is the best possible system. The strong should thrive and control the society and the weak should be powerless and die early, according to our Kahn beliefs. But that assumes that the strong act in their-own best interest. The critical component is here." Nin pointed to a timeline on the graph. "We convince the population to vote against their own best interest. They begin to elect corrupt and incompetent government officials that start tearing down the government services that strengthen the country. To do that, we move wealth from the middle class to the wealthy."

Keo's anger was visible but controlled. His mind went into an attack mode. His solution for handling people who disagreed with him was to attack and destroy them while he maintained the appearance that he was a patriotic citizen being forced to do the right thing. He began thinking of ways to destroy Nin, and if necessary, kill him.

Nin looked directly at Keo. He dared not tell him that he was missing a key point. He chose his words carefully. "The key element is that the wealthy are brainwashed as well. They ignore science and the experts. They are so totally focused on making short term gains by any means that they ignore all other concerns. They view themselves as hard-working risk takers even though they hire others to do the research and they don't take significant risks. They view themselves as patriotic even though they don't give much thought as to what they can do for their country. They refuse to pay taxes for all the government services that helped make them rich. They view themselves as super-intelligent and assume the lower classes are too stupid or lazy to make money or even to survive."

Nin stopped himself. He knew he was on dangerous territory. Too much information would get him into more trouble with Keo. He waited for Keo to respond. Keo looked at the graphs. "I see. The wealthy are brainwashed as well. In a free-market system they make their money by being more intelligent than others and they make the important decisions. They control the society. So you are saying we set up a wealthy ruling class that unknowingly destroys their economy. Can you do that?"

Nin let out a long sigh and closed his eyes. His death had been seconds away and he knew he had literally dodged a bullet with his words. More importantly, he thought there was a chance Keo might support his plan. "Yes. We set up a news organization that the wealthy always watch. We call it 'The Right News', or something like that. We use religion and bright patriotic colors, charts and tables and do selective reporting.

We select or fabricate news that attacks science and government. If something bad happens it's always the government that is to blame. Something good is always done by the wealthy even if it's done by the middle class. We appeal to their emotions and their egos. It takes time but it will work. And we have time."

"How can you be so sure it will work?"

"There are all kinds of scientific Earth studies that show how to brainwash people. You know from your work on Earth how suggestible these humans can be."

Keo looked at the charts. "What's this alternative plan?"

Nin looked at it. "That's where we move wealth from the wealthy to the middle class. The middle class grows in size until the planet's resources are used up. The population explodes. Global warming, pollution, food and water shortages wreak havoc on the species. Wars result. I can reevaluate it if you want, but the computer models are not as accurate with this timeline. Unpredictable paths may evolve due to the increased chances of aberrations occurring in a large, educated middle-class population. There is a chance they could solve their own problems with this approach and be strong enough to destroy us before we land. If they don't solve their own problems they may be weak when we arrive but we might end up with an uninhabitable planet."

Keo looked at the summaries for the two different options. "Your first plan has a 98.7% chance of success according to your computer model and we get a clean planet. The numbers indicate we should go with this plan. It's too bad not to use the most powerful army in the universe against them. I'm proud to say that my companies built the Mallat robots. They are such sweetly engineered killing machines. Your idea to program the Mallat with religion was ingenious.

Our kill rate grew exponentially when we did that. They never questioned their orders. In ten years the Krat will be nothing but a memory of their annoying pleas for help. In twenty years even those memories will be forgotten."

Keo thought for a moment and then said with a spark of energy in his eyes. "We can still use the Mallat robots, can't we? I mean we don't want to make the same mistake again that we made on our planet. We put the Krats in survival camps where they bred diseases, which ultimately infected our own people. This time we will put these humans in survival camps and exterminate them immediately, before they have a chance to breed diseases. I'll go with your plan, Nin. But let me make it clear; I don't like you. You make one mistake and I'll make sure it will be your last. I want to see results. Are we clear on that?"

Nin knew how powerful Keo's companies were and that they had developed and produced the Mallat. Nin had warned Keo during the Kahn-Krat wars that religious and patriotic robots like the Mallat would be ruthless and his computer models could not predict what might happen if they were utilized. He was pleased Keo had acknowledged his skills and given tentative support to his plans. He was relieved he didn't have to take his plan to the council for approval without Keo's support. Even over the great distance between the spaceship and the Kahn planet, Keo was still very powerful and could easily arrange Nin's death.

There was much more in the computer models that Nin did not want to reveal. Some of the paths puzzled Nin. Most of them lead to Nin's punishment and death. His first priority was to avoid those paths at all cost. "Yes, Keo, I understand. I'll implement the plan as soon as the council authorizes it," Nin said, as Keo's holographic image disappeared.

4

THE TROUBLE WITH POL

After Joe finished viewing the video Pol had taken of the faculty-student gathering at the president's house, Joe realized he didn't know how much Pol could understand. Pol had seemed more human lately. Sometimes Joe thought Pol was putting emotional tones in his sentences. He almost detected some compassion in what Pol said next. "I've found Jazz Jones' computer on the network. She is checking her social media accounts now."

"What? Why would she be online this late at night?"

Pol did not answer. Perhaps he did not understand the question or perhaps he did not know the answer.

"Do you want me to send a message to her?" Pol asked.

"Yes. I mean, say 'I noticed you were online. Just wondering what you were doing up so late.'"

A few minutes later Pol read back Jazz's text message. "Sojo, I should ask you the same question. I just finished studying so I decided to see who's online. I know you aren't studying for class tomorrow. Have you come up with any bizarre physics questions yet?"

"Tell her, 'I had a dream and it woke me up. You were in it.'"

After a long pause her answer came back, "Call me."

Pol said in his monotone voice, "Are you going to call her?"

Joe nodded and dialed the number on his cell phone. He

told Jazz the entire dream. They talked until four in the morning. And when they hung up, sleep did not come easily to Joe. He didn't tell her much about Pol. She assumed that Pol was just an imaginary character in his dream. When she asked him about the entanglement project, he told her only what she could find out herself online. He told her it was Einstein's thought experiment designed to prove that quantum theory was flawed because immediate action at a distance was impossible. However when the experiment was actually performed it proved that immediate action at a distance really does happen. He mentioned he was interested in large-scale quantum entanglement. She pressed him no further on the issue.

Joe rarely used an alarm clock. He usually woke up early. However the lack of sleep the previous night and the previous night's conversation left him dazed when it was time to get up for his 9 AM class. Pol's mechanical voice finally woke him up five minutes before class. "Will you be getting up this morning, Joe?"

Joe answered "yes", but then turned over to catch just a few minutes more rest.

"Class is in five minutes," Pol stated in his monotone voice.

Joe jumped up. "What? You should have gotten me up earlier."

"I am afraid I overslept as well, and I've been thinking about what we experienced." Pol used "sleep" as a time to generate and test new thoughts in highly unstructured settings. When Pol was working on particularly difficult problems, he sometimes "slept" more.

"No time. We can talk about that later." Joe scrambled to find his clothes.

"You will never make it to class in time. It is snowing outside. I estimate you will miss the first 15 minutes."

"So much for getting a B in that class... I thought you were programmed to help me get better grades."

"Wait... Wait please. Yes. The class is in the multi-media room. I can access the camera in the back and you will be able to see and hear the lecture from your laptop, so you do not need to go to class."

"Do it."

Professor Anthony Neil's Monday lecture was on the quantum mechanics of heavier nuclei. He always left ten minutes at the end of his lectures for questions. As usual Jazz asked questions that summarized the lecture and helped Joe understand the theory. Her last question startled Joe.

"How does large-scale quantum entanglement affect these calculations?"

Professor Neil looked at Jazz curiously. "What do you mean, Miss Jones?"

Joe jumped up from his chair. "Pol, can you text her now?"

"Yes. She always has her laptop on during class. Yes. I found it."

Joe didn't bother to ask Pol how he found Jazz's computer or how he knew she always had it on in class. "Have her say, 'I've been meaning to ask that question several lectures back but never found the opportunity.'"

Jazz hesitated as she looked curiously at her computer. "Joe Abre was wondering if large-scale quantum entanglement might explain some real world directly observable phenomena.'"

"No!" Joe yelled at his computer. "Don't ask it for me. Now he'll know I skipped his class!"

Professor Neil looked shocked. The question seemed to confuse him. The fact that Joe Abre was not in his classroom did not help. "I don't see Mr. Abre."

"Can I talk to him through the AV link?" Joe asked Pol.

"I'm sorry, Joe," Pol apologized. The speakers are off and I can't control them. The only way to communicate with him is by texting Jazz."

"Tell Jazz I am monitoring the class through the AV camera and to tell Professor Neil." Joe watched on the screen as the scene played out.

Professor Neil continued to look confused. "I'm not sure why Mr. Abre chose to be a virtual student today. I'll check with department policy on that later. In any case Mr. Abre, I'd like to know why you're asking such a far-fetched question." The professor then looked down at his cell phone and read a text message.

When Joe was about to respond Professor Neil shocked him by requesting to see him later. "Please come to my office at four this afternoon, Mister Abre. Bring your real self this time." Then he shocked Jazz. "Miss Jones. Please take the rest of the questions on this lecture and homework. I have something urgent to do."

He left the room leaving Joe and Jazz confused. Jazz slowly stood up and provided answers to all the questions that came up. Joe was impressed with her. He was convinced that she could teach the class and probably would be a professor in a few years if she wanted. More importantly he wondered if he was in trouble.

Later that day at noon Jazz found Joe in the Union computer cluster. Jazz looked at him curiously. "You overslept, didn't you?"

"I didn't mean to."

"I doubt anyone intends to oversleep. But that's not what bothers me."

The way she said that alarmed him. Great. He thought. Now I am in trouble with Jazz, too.

"I checked the multi-media support room behind the classroom after class. It was locked and there wasn't a tech person there. I also did not have my texting program turned on. How is it that you can control my computer?"

5

A TIME TO TELL SECRETS

Jazz looked down at Joe as he was sitting at one of the computers in the Union computer lounge and demanded an answer from him. He had to tell her the truth or he would lose whatever relationship he had with her. "I didn't. I mean I can't control your computer, at least not directly."

Jazz looked at him curiously. She had been prepared to leave if she determined he had hacked into her computer. For some reason she trusted him, at least enough to hear an imaginative answer.

"Ok," Joe said, "I'm going to tell you something I haven't told anyone else. I'm hoping you can keep it a secret."

"I can't promise anything. Have you done something illegal?"

Joe looked down. "I don't know. But if the college finds out, I could get kicked out. I never meant for it to happen. I thought you already had your text program on when I sent the message."

"That doesn't make sense. Tell me what you've done and then I'll tell you if I can keep a secret."

Joe hesitated. Jazz held his arms so that he looked up at her. "Tell me or I'm leaving. I'll have lunch somewhere else."

"No. Wait. I created something, something that has helped me with my courses. I call it Pol. It stands for Physics of Learning. It's a program that is intelligent. It's developed into something like a real person which I can't control. I asked Pol to contact you and he did. I didn't realize he had to start your text program to do it."

Jazz let go of his arms. "You mean the Pol in your dream? You are trying to tell me that you've really created artificial intelligence and you have no control over it? And you think you will get kicked out of school for doing something that has baffled scientist and engineers for decades? Well, I knew you were creative. I just didn't expect you to make up such an imaginative lie, a lie that doesn't even make sense. I thought you were smarter than that."

Jazz started to leave. Joe stood up. "No, Jazz, please." Joe took off his glasses and handed them to Jazz. "Put these on."

"Why?"

"Just do it. Please."

Jazz removed her glasses and put on Joe's and said, "I don't see anything unusual."

"Your voice sounds odd, Jazz." Pol's voice echoed in her head. "It's not you. It's me. I'm adjusting for it. Say something else."

Jazz sat down with her hands holding the glasses just in case she wanted to take them off quickly. "Who are you?"

"Don't do that," Pol replied. "Don't touch the glasses. That distorts the sensor readings. Say something else."

Jazz lowered her hands slowly and looked off into the distance. She asked, "Are you real? I mean are you someone playing a joke on me?"

"That's better. Do I sound okay? I can adjust for that too. I am real. I'm not human, but I am real. Do I sound okay?"

Jazz didn't know what to think. She looked around the room for someone with a microphone pretending to be Pol. "You sound fine. If you are just a computer program, why is Joe worried about telling people about you?"

"You don't have to speak out loud. You can just whisper if you want. Joe doesn't even have to whisper his words anymore. I've learned to understand his words from his brain waves. We've implemented adaptive nano-electronics. I will learn how to do that with you as well. You know you are only the second person I have ever talked to. I wasn't sure how the sensors would work with someone else. "

"Answer my question please," Jazz whispered. "If you are just a computer program, why is Joe worried about having people find out about you?"

"Joe thinks it is not fair that I help him with his courses. I have taken some liberties with accessing other computers. I didn't know it was wrong. Joe told me to stop and I have. I am sorry that I opened your text program."

Jazz hesitated. "I don't understand. Did you help Joe cheat on tests?"

"Before I became aware of myself and time, I did help him on open-book exams. Was that wrong? My main purpose is to help Joe with his courses. Was that wrong?"

Jazz wasn't sure how to respond. "Did you do anything else that you think might be wrong?"

"I did help Joe with writing papers and doing homework problems. You don't like me because you think I am getting Joe in trouble?"

Jazz leaned back. "I don't know you, so I can't say if I like you or not."

"I don't understand. You know Joe, so you know me."

"I'm going to talk with Joe now." Jazz took the glasses off and looked at Joe who was sitting in the chair looking down.

Jazz touched his arm. "Joe. He's in your head all of the time. That's kind of weird."

Joe looked at her. "You get used to it. He's usually pretty

quiet. What did he say?"

She handed the glasses back to Joe. "Leave them off. He thinks I don't like him."

"Really, he never said that before. He's been evolving lately, getting more emotional."

"I assume the glasses are connected by a wireless connection to some computer. What kind of computer is he running on?"

Joe looked around at all the computers in the lounge and remained silent.

Jazz eyes opened wider. "You didn't?"

Joe looked down nodding his head. "Pol runs on any networked computer that is not being used for something else."

Jazz sat down next to him. "Pol is the reason my computer runs slowly?"

Joe shook his head. "No. Pol gets off your computer as soon as you use it. It's all the other network garbage that's been slowing everyone's computers. Besides I've been purchasing more computers to support Pol's CPU time."

Jazz looked at him not knowing what to think. "How can you afford high-end computers and high-tech glasses?"

"Pol has been studying the stock market. We've been using Google search trends to anticipate consumer purchasing patterns. We've profited on some investments. It's a slow process but we've made enough to purchase what we need for the computers and the adaptive nanoelectronics."

Jazz studied him and then looked at the glasses. "I don't know what to think about this, Joe. You may be in more trouble than I thought. What else have you done with Pol?"

"He helps me with the entanglement project I told you about. He records everything I see and hear. Do you think Pol will get me in trouble?"

Jazz thought about it. "Yes and no. It sounds like you used him on exams and to write papers. It's weird that he is in your head all the time and that when I'm talking to you, there is this other person-like thing watching and listening. On the other hand, you've accomplished something great here." Jazz hesitated. "You are not playing a joke on me, are you? I mean Pol isn't some real person at the other end. Why does he want to know if I like him? I wouldn't expect an artificial intelligence program to be concerned with being liked by me."

Joe thought about it. "I don't know why he wants you to like him."

"He did secretly help you with open-book exams and writing papers. But I think you are okay. Most professors would just be pleased you developed an amazing AI program. Maybe in the future all students will have their own personal AI program helping them with their studies."

"I have to see Professor Neil at four today. I can't tell him Pol hacked into the AV room computer so I could watch his lecture. What do I tell him?"

"Personally, I don't know what to think. Pol hacked into my computer and apparently he's been listening to our conversations without my knowledge. That's all just too creepy. I need time to think about this. I do know I want this stuff to stop now! That means you, Pol," Jazz told the glasses that Joe held in his hand.

Jazz looked down at Joe. "I think you should just tell Professor Neil the truth and hope for the best." She then walked away leaving Joe to think he had just lost something very important.

6

PROFESSOR ANTHONY NEIL

Joe knocked timidly on Professor Neil's door. He hoped that Professor Neil had forgotten about the meeting and wasn't in his office, that all of his problems would disappear if he ignored them. His hopes were dashed as he heard Professor Neil's voice. "Come in."

Professor Neil was at his computer working on something that seemed important. He raised his index figure gesturing Joe to wait. He was shaking his head from time to time and mumbling to himself: "Unbelievable, just unbelievable."

Joe hoped he wasn't looking at his grades on the screen.

Finally Professor Neil looked at Joe and then reached for an exam that was sitting on his desk. Joe recognized his writing and he saw a grade of C+ on the exam. Neil flipped through it to the third page. "I've been meaning to ask you about this. You've derived some equations in the margin here. What's that all about?"

Joe looked at the page. "I'm sorry, professor, I couldn't remember the equations for relativity, so I derived them in the margin. I should have memorized them."

Neil looked at the equations. "You derived them from scratch. We didn't cover that in class. I just gave you the final equations. Did you derive them before?"

Joe was puzzled. "No. That's the first time I had to derive them. I'm afraid it took more time than I thought it would. I didn't have time to answer the last two questions."

Neil nodded as he looked over the derivation. "You derived Einstein's special relativity equations in less than an hour." Neil put the exam down. "And now you are interested in large scale quantum entanglement?"

Joe looked at him. The conversation was going in a different direction than he had anticipated and he was unsure where it would lead. "I…" Joe paused, not sure what Professor Neil wanted to hear. He remembered what Jazz had said about just telling the truth and hoping for the best. "I've been wondering if quantum entangled crystals might exhibit observable quantum entanglement effects."

Neil's eyes opened wider. "Well, you could say I've been wondering about that too. How far have you got?"

"Not very, I'm bogged down with the equations."

"Yes, they are challenging. But I'll tell you what. I want to hire you as a research assistant working for me. You'll have complete freedom to research this topic. Every week we'll get together at this time and we'll discuss what you've done and make plans for what to do next. How does that sound?"

Joe was shocked. "I don't know what to say. That sounds great. But I do already have teaching assistant responsibilities."

"Don't worry about that. We'll have one of the other graduate students take over your responsibilities. I'll take care of that this afternoon with a phone call to the physics office. You'll be paid a little more too." Neil stood up. "Unfortunately, I've got to attend a meeting in Boston this evening. It's about something amazing and I don't want to miss my plane." Neil grabbed his briefcase and stuffed some papers into it. "You can reach me anytime by email or by my cell phone. "Neil grabbed a piece of paper, looked at it, and put it in his pocket. He grabbed another piece and wrote his cell phone number on it and handed it to Joe.

"Don't hesitate to call, Joe. I'm always available at this number. I want to keep very close tabs on your progress. Call anytime. I'll be back on Wednesday for our class. Just lock the door on your way out."

Joe remained seated as Neil rushed out the door. At first he felt like he had dodged a bullet. Then he felt like he had won the lottery. He went over Neil's words in his mind to make sure he had understood them correctly. Did Professor Neil really just offer him a paid research assistant position? There was no other way to interpret what Neil had said. Joe was going to get paid for something he enjoyed doing; something he would have done on his own in his spare time.

Joe wondered if Pol had been listening. "Pol, did you just hear what I heard?" he asked.

"Hi Joe, there was no way I was going to miss this meeting. I thought you might have to tell him about me. Instead he just hired you to work with him on your entanglement project and he's going to pay you more money. Does that mean we can do another upgrade on the glasses?"

"Yes, I believe it does," Joe said, as he got up slowly and looked around Professor Neil's office. It was a typical professor's office with a desk and shelves cluttered with books and papers. Except for several pictures and statues of dolphins and the fact he had just hired a student with a C average to do research, Neil seemed like a normal professor. Joe walked cautiously out of the office as if he might suddenly lose his balance. He closed and locked the door on his way out. As soon as he got back to his apartment, he sent Jazz an email describing what had happened. He didn't know if she would respond, but he felt he had to share his good news with her.

7

JAZZ JONES

Professor Neil did not show up for his Wednesday class with Joe and Jazz. After ten minutes, one of the students asked Jazz to explain one of the homework problems due that day. Jazz started to explain the problem from her desk, but with encouragement from other students in the class, she got up and explained the rest of the problem at the board. Several more questions came up about the lecture topic scheduled for that day. Jazz ended up giving an entire lecture complete with a ten minute question and answer session on the assigned homework problems.

At the end of the lecture when everyone except Joe and Jazz had left, Joe began to chuckle.

"What? Did I miss something?" Jazz asked as she looked over her notes.

"No. It's just that I think you should be teaching the class. You covered all the material and you answered my questions before I could ask them. You made a really difficult subject very easy to understand."

"I'm such a nerd, aren't I?"

"No, not at all," Joe paused for a few seconds. "Well yes, you are, but in a good way. The class is lucky to have you to go over this for us."

"It helps me too, you know. Teaching is the best way to learn. You think of all kinds of aspects of the material that you would otherwise overlook. So I have to thank you for listening."

Joe enjoyed looking at her. Her glasses did nothing to prevent him from getting lost in her charms. Joe thought to himself, *she's beautiful, athletic and brilliant. I'm not in the same league with her. How could I ever think she might like me?*

Jazz sensed his thoughts. "Look Joe. I've been thinking. I like you. It's just that this Pol thing takes some getting used to. I think we can be friends, but nothing more." She paused, wondering how to say the things she thought she had to say. She sat down in the chair next to Joe.

Joe sat back in his chair.

"I don't have time for a relationship. I came here to get my doctorate, pretty much against my parent's wishes. They wanted me to stay in Boston. I just wanted to get away from them, to lead my own life. In any case, my music courses lowered my GPA so much that it limited my college choices, so I chose a smaller university. I need to do really well so I can find a job where I can do something great as a physicist. I need to get all A's here and do some outstanding research. Does that make any sense?"

Joe didn't say anything so Jazz continued. "Remember the swing, Joe. In seventh grade, I used to go to the playground a lot with a boy named Charlie. He kept asking me to kiss him. I finally gave in. We went under the slide."

Joe leaned forward. "What happened?"

"Absolutely nothing... We kissed. I went back to my swing and he stopped going to the playground with me."

"So you now avoid any kind of relationships because some kid in seventh grade got what he wanted and stopped playing with you?"

"Yes and no." Jazz answered. "That's just one example. You see, there is something about me. When I was skipping those music classes in college, I spent the time partying. I had a few relationships. Every one of them ended the same way. People leave me when they get what they want. Everything changed when I started doing what I wanted, when I started focusing on what I am good at, studying physics. I'm a lot happier now."

"So you think I'll forget about you if we get more serious?"

"I guess. I don't know. I'm just happier now that I'm focusing on what's important. You understand, don't you?"

Joe thought to himself, *she's dumping me even before we have any kind of relationship, and she's doing it in the nicest way she can. I guess the Pol thing was too much. But at least she cares about my feelings and we can still be friends.*

"You figured out what you really want and you're going after it with everything you have, no matter what," Joe said and then paused while he collected his thoughts. "Sometimes you learn more by following the less obvious path. You wanted to get away from your parents. They wanted you to be a great musician, but that's not who you are. You are something else entirely. You're worried you're disappointing them. You don't need that distraction, so you moved away from them."

"One of the hardest things to do in life is change," Joe continued. "We get comfortable with the way things are. You woke up one day and you realized the life you were living wasn't the one you wanted. You found the courage and the energy to change. I admire that. But you still have to keep your eyes open in this new life of yours. Life is not a simple program that you follow from beginning to end with a fixed set of rules. Books and studying are important, but happiness and the answers you are looking for sometimes come from where you least expect it. What I'm trying to say is there will always be other opportunities waiting for you."

Joe looked at Jazz. He realized that spoken words have little value unless someone hears them and accepts their meaning. "Jazz, I can only tell you what I know. You will be great at whatever you choose to do."

"You sound like my parents. They say that, but then there is always a pause, like they're thinking, 'You let us down. You didn't try hard enough at music.'"

Joe leaned forward. "Look, you are too amazing a person for me to ever forget. I'm just glad we can be friends."

Joe leaned back after an awkward pause. "Why did you choose this college out of all the other colleges out there?"

Jazz looked at her notes, eager to change the subject. "Professor Neil's publications on quantum physics attracted my attention. There is something about him that's different, like he knows things that others don't. Sometimes you get a professor who doesn't completely understand the material. They usually make their lectures much more complicated than needed. Professor Neil is the opposite. I came here to take courses from him and hopefully to do research with him. I don't understand why I get straight A's, and yet he hires you to be his research assistant."

Jazz looked down. "Don't get me wrong, Joe. I'm happy for you. I see why he picked you. But I don't have what you have. I guess it's not enough to get straight A's."

Joe smiled. "I think an opportunity just popped up for you. Let's work on this project together. Professor Neil gave me complete control over this research. I'll tell Professor Neil that I need you to help me. You can come to our meetings. He may not want to pay you, but that doesn't matter. The money's not important. I'll pay you. Frankly, I desperately need your help with it."

Jazz hadn't thought about that possibility. That could work. Professor Neil had asked her to finish his lecture. He must have confidence in her. A smile began to grow on her face. "Do you think he would agree to that?"

"I think so." And after he thought about it more, he said, "I'll make him agree to it."

Jazz wanted to hug Joe, but she stopped herself. "I can't afford to have any kind of relationship, Joe. It will take a lot of hard work and time to do this research. We would have to work really hard and stay focused. You understand, don't you?"

Joe sat back again. "That's what I like about you. You are driven to learn, a true force of nature." He let out a laugh. "You are such a nerd."

Jazz sat back and laughed. "We're both nerds."

Joe became serious. "Ok, so let's start right now. Professor Neil was extremely interested in quantum entanglement. Remember it was that question on large scale effects of quantum entanglement that intrigued him."

Jazz sat back, thumbed through her notes and smiled. "Yes, and the fact that you weren't in his class when you asked the question."

Joe smiled and continued talking. "So what do you know about quantum teleportation?"

Jazz had just read a paper on it. "It's impossible on any practical scale. It's been proven to occur in the lab with photons and other particles, but so far no experiment has shown that information can travel faster than the speed of light."

Joe asked. "Why is it impossible on a large scale?"

Jazz thought for a second. "Well, thermal noise will drown out any observable effects."

"Ok. So let's put everything at zero degrees Kelvin."

"That's the problem. If you want to teleport something across a room, you can't put the entire room at zero degrees."

"That's true," Joe nodded, "but maybe you just have to put the sending component and the receiving component at low temperatures."

Jazz thoughts began to race. She wasn't sure if that would work. "Ok. Maybe…"

Joe went on. "And maybe you don't even have to lower the temperature. What do you know about superconductors? What if entanglement could be used to make room-temperature superconductors?"

Jazz's eyes widened. "No. That can't be right. Can it?" Jazz thought for a few minutes. "So you are saying make two entangled crystals each encased in a room-temperature superconducting shield. You need to get everything in the same quantum state…," Jazz's thoughts raced.

Joe waited a few seconds. "That's my hunch and that's as far as I got. I can't do the quantum equations. Can you do it?"

Jazz's smile brought a renewed sense of energy to Joe. "I was born to do this," she said.

The conversation went on through lunch. In a few hours Jazz, with help from Joe and Pol, had worked through the large scale quantum entanglement equations that enabled two people to communicate with each other not only across a room but across the entire universe with two small superconducting crystals. None of them could have done it alone but together they felt they could do anything.

Jazz felt like they had just scaled the highest mountain. "We have to show this to Professor Neil."

Joe was excited but more cautious. "We don't know if this will work. I don't even know if it can be done in the lab. How do we make a room-temperature superconducting crystal? And how do you test them to see if we can communicate information across space faster than the speed of light? There are so many questions."

The feeling of accomplishment made Jazz giddy. She had never been so happy. "It's all in the equations, Joe. It works so beautifully on paper that it's got to work in reality. I'm positive we can do this in the lab." She laughed and hugged Joe.

Joe couldn't help but laugh with her. He thought about how special she was. How many people in the world could get so elated deriving a bunch of equations? He realized he had fallen in love with a very beautiful and unique person who was way out of his league and just wanted him as a friend. Still, he tried to convince himself, it's enough just to make her happy.

"We'll show this to Professor Neil and he'll help us with the lab experiments," Jazz said, as she let go of Joe and looked at the paper with the equations. Caught up in the moment of discovery, she was oblivious to Joe's thoughts.

8
TROUBLE

Joe couldn't reach Professor Neil by email or by phone, so he and Jazz looked forward to seeing him in class on Friday. After the first ten minutes of the class, they realized that Neil was not going to show up. Once again, some of the students asked Jazz questions about the homework assignment and Jazz ended up giving them a lecture on the material assigned for Friday's lecture. At one point, Jazz suggested that it was someone else's turn to answer questions, but no one else dared to discuss the material; no one else could do what Jazz could do.

Professor Neil was known for sticking to his syllabus. This material would be on the test in two weeks and they had all decided Jazz was the only person who could help them learn it.

After the lecture, Jazz asked Joe, "Where is he?"

Joe looked up from his notes. "I know. He said he would be here today. He said he could always be reached by email or by cell phone. Something's wrong. Let's check with the Department Chair."

Doctor Ryder, the Department Chair, told them that she had been trying to reach Professor Neil since Tuesday and that she would let them know as soon as she heard from him. The Chair, a kind but serious lady, said she hoped nothing was wrong with him. "Just in case he's not back on Monday, I'm working on getting a substitute professor for the course. You'll definitely have a professor on Monday."

Joe and Jazz went to the computer room in the Union and Joe sat down and said, "I don't believe it. Even if he was sick, he would still answer his cell phone or at least reply to our messages. Pol has searched all of the hotels in the area and all of the police reports. It's like Professor Neil just vanished off the planet after he got off his plane in Boston."

Jazz looked at Joe and his glasses. "Did Pol record your meeting with him?"

Pol, who was listening to the conversation through Joe's glasses, told Joe, "I did, but I didn't see anything out of the ordinary. He looked fine to me."

"Pol, can you play it back?" Joe asked out loud so Jazz could hear.

Pol put the video of the meeting with Professor Neil on the computer in front of Joe. They watched it several times from beginning to end until Jazz noticed something at the end of the meeting. "There. That piece of paper he put in his pocket. Can you have Pol zoom in on it?"

Pol could hear Jazz's words through Joe's glasses and immediately zoomed in on the paper.

Joe looked at it closely. "There are words on it but I can't make it out."

They both focused on the screen, and then Jazz said, "I can't either. Pol, I want you to combine all of the video frames you have of that paper. Orient and size them so they are on top of each other. Can you do that?"

The answer came fairly quickly as Pol stacked each image of the paper. Suddenly the words became readable.

"Boston, Meeting of Planets, 8 PM, 10/27/08, 231 Stodder Drive, Betty Rowe"

Joe and Jazz both read out loud the part "Meeting of Planets."

"I never heard of that," Joe said.

Jazz started to Google it on the computer next to her.

Joe stopped her. "Pol's already done it." Joe repeated what Pol had just told him. "There is nothing that's related so far. Just some religious references to the birth of Jesus, and another one to Santa Claus…"

Jazz looked down at the carpeted floor, deep in thought. Finally she looked up. "Can Pol get Betty Rowe's telephone number?"

Joe gestured with his finger for Jazz to wait while Pol looked it up.

After several minutes, Pol responded in a text message through the computer in front of them. "That's strange. There is no information on a Betty Rowe living on or near Stodder Drive in Boston. I don't think she exists."

Jazz looked at Joe. "Or she doesn't want anyone to know she exists."

"Pol is very good at finding information. People leave all kinds of trails on the internet." Joe replied. "She would have to be very good at covering up all of her activity. Pol, does 231 Stodder Drive exist?"

Pol told Joe it did and Joe nodded to Jazz.

"We have to go there, Joe. We'll go see this Betty Rowe. We've got to find out what happened to him."

Joe couldn't say no to her. This was important, not only to make sure Professor Neil was okay, but also to make sure they could continue their research. They thought they had just discovered something very important about large-scale quantum entanglement and they couldn't wait any longer to show their results to Professor Neil.

"Another grad student is taking over my teaching responsibilities," Joe said, "so I'm free this afternoon. Do you have anything?"

"I've got a lab I have to teach, but I'm pretty sure I can get Sally to teach it. She practically begged me to tutor her in our quantum class. We should be able to work out something. I've also got an intramural basketball game Saturday morning. They'll miss me, but this is much more important."

"We can take my car," Joe said. "If we leave now we can make it there by five. I'll stop by my apartment first and then I'll pick you up in front of your dorm in half an hour."

A half hour later, they were heading to Boston. Joe reached into the glove compartment and handed Jazz a small rectangular box. "I've got a present for you."

Jazz took the box and turned it around in her hands. Her first thought was that she wanted to avoid any kind of relationship. "I can't, Joe. We've got to stay focused."

"It's not what you think. Open it. I'll understand if you don't want it."

Jazz hesitated. "It's not a bracelet or necklace or something, is it? If it's a harmonica, I'm going to throw it out the window." She slowly opened the box as Joe drove on. She lifted the cover and said, "You got me a pair of glasses?"

"I did try to match your glasses, but these are not just ordinary glasses. Put them on."

Jazz removed her glasses and put on the new pair. Pol's voice greeted her. "Hello, Jazz. Do you like me now?"

"I like the idea that Joe made these glasses for me." Jazz looked at Joe. "Thank you Joe. I do like them."

"I had a bunch of spare parts, so I made some extra glasses. I just thought you might be getting tired of watching me talk to Pol without knowing what we are saying. Now you can join in the conversation."

"I was wondering what you two were saying about me.

Thank you, Joe," she said, as she kissed him on the cheek.

9

CONFRONTATION

Betty Rowe's house was a typical house, in a typical upper class neighborhood located just outside of Boston. The large front lawn and walkway leading to the front door gave no clue as to what they would discover in the house.

Jazz knocked on the front door. Betty Rowe answered the door and stared at them coldly. Joe was stunned by how much she resembled Jazz. They could have been sisters. But the resemblance made the differences in them striking. Rowe wore makeup and a black short skirt with a low-cut white top. She had the icy indifferent stare of a fashion model walking down a runway. Whereas Jazz's eyes and mannerisms revealed a fascination and thirst for life, Rowe's eyes revealed a rigid calculated focus. If looks could kill, Rowe would have been declared a master at the technique. Joe had the eerie feeling that this woman could easily kill without feeling any kind of emotion or regret. Her sexual beauty and coldness reminded him of a flame on a cold night attracting a moth to its death.

Roe's stare stopped Joe and Jazz cold. "What do you want?"

They couldn't find the words to answer so Rowe continued, "I don't have time for this." Rowe began to close the door.

Jazz found her words. "Wait. We're trying to find our professor, Anthony Neil. This is Joe Abre and I'm Jazz Jones."

Roe stopped instantly. Her eyes went back to assessing

them. She went into her house leaving the door open so they could follow. They followed her into a large dining room area that had been converted into an office. Shelves of old and new books lined the walls. Some of the shelves held stacks of old newspapers. A large desk placed in the center room supported several large computer monitors. All of them were displaying various types of graphs and news articles.

"Did Anthony Neil tell you about me?" Rowe asked Joe.

Jazz noticed Professor Neil's briefcase lying precariously on the floor next to the desk as if someone had just been rifling through it. It was the same one he brought to all of his classes. She covered her mouth and whispered to Joe and Pol through her glasses. "Professor Neil's briefcase is here. I'm going to search the house."

"I'm sorry," Jazz said out loud to Rowe. "It's been a long trip here. Could I use your bathroom?"

Joe studied Rowe's face. She stared into the distance as if she was doing some type of calculation. Her expression was blank and unreadable. She led Jazz down a hall and opened a door for Jazz and told her to come right back after she was done.

Jazz went in the bathroom and closed the door behind her. She listened at the door to Rowe's footsteps walking down the hall. Then she quietly opened the door a crack and waited for Rowe to return to Joe.

Joe looked around the room. Some of the books and newspapers dated back to the 1940's, yet the latest computer technology covered her desk.

Joe returned his gaze to the bookshelves as Rowe came back and sat down at the desk. "I inherited this house from my father." That iron stare focused on Joe again and she repeated her question. "Did Anthony Neil tell you about me?"

"No. I saw your name on his desk before he vanished. I thought you might know where he went."

"Vanished? No. He had to do some research or attend a conference, I believe. The college should know where he is. You shouldn't jump to conclusions or say things that imply something bad has happened."

"So he is fine?"

"Yes, I am sure he is."

"When was the last time you saw him?"

"Enough questions from you. Neil said some interesting things about you. Did he tell you about his interstellar communication project?"

"Interstellar? He never mentioned anything like that."

Hearing Joe's conversation with Rowe, Jazz stepped into the hallway, quietly closed the bathroom door behind her and began examining the house.

Roe looked at Joe curiously. "Very well, let's discuss something else. I am an environmentalist. I've been wondering about how to save the Earth from global warming and all of the other damage the human species is wreaking on this planet. I've concluded that the only way to stop the damage is to bring about an economic depression. I'm just speaking hypothetically, of course. If you had the means, how would you create an economic depression?"

Joe was stunned by the change of topic. But he thought he would have to play along so he could glean more information about Professor Neil from her. "Ahh… I wouldn't. I don't even want to think about that. Depressions can bring about wars, suffering and death."

Roe looked down the hall where Jazz had gone. Joe realized he was going to have to stall Rowe to give Jazz a chance to explore the house.

"Well. If it's just hypothetical, I would go back to the fundamentals I learned in economics class. I suppose if you disrupt supply and demand cycles somehow, you could create an economic depression."

"I don't want a mediocre answer. I want you to think outside the box. Neil said you think differently than others. If that's all you have, then you and your friend must go. I'm very busy. There is a presidential election coming up in four days and I have a lot to do."

"No, wait." Economics was one of the few courses Joe aced in college. He didn't know why. He never liked the idea of thinking of real people as just consumers and producers. People were more than variables in an equation. Still, the economic relationships were easy for him to understand and he didn't have to study much to do well on the tests.

"I always thought the parameters of supply and demand made the economic model too confined. I thought motivation was also important."

"Go on."

"Supply and demand applies only to products. Motivation in a society to do something, tells you about future products that don't exist yet. So you measure how motivated people are to do something, anything…, and that's the precursor to new supply and demand cycles."

"And how does that relate to economic depressions?"

"You're asking me how one person could create an economic depression. They couldn't if they merely tried to disrupt current supply and demand cycles. The motivation for those cycles already exists. If you disrupt them, new ones will take their place."

Roe looked at a drawer in her desk. Pol noticed Rowe's gaze and warned Joe silently through his glasses to be cautious.

"Joe. There is something very wrong here. I sense a local radio signal that is not right."

Joe wasn't sure how to proceed. So he went with his rule. When in doubt, just say what you think. "I would look at what motivates a society. There are obvious things like advertising. There are basic things like health, food, shelter and security. There is love, greed, materialism, fear and hate."

"I don't see where you are going with this." Again, she looked at the drawer.

The pressure was on him to come up with an idea, any idea to stall her from kicking them out. How could one person take down the world economy? This was like a question on an exam and he was running out of time. He said the first two words that came into his head and hoped he could follow up with an explanation.

"Parasitic Wealth!" His mind raced through ways to explain these words. Suddenly he realized it was like a trick question. "You see. There is no way one person can create an economic depression. But there is a motivation that already exists and could be reinforced to destroy the economy. Let's call it Parasitic Wealth."

Roe's hand made a small movement to the drawer in her desk, and then withdrew. Joe did not understand it. He had an answer to the question. What could be in the drawer? What would Rowe pull out of the drawer if Joe's answer was right, or wrong?

"There are those in society whose main goal is the accumulation of wealth and power," Joe continued. Society expects them to make sound investments with their wealth that benefit not just them but the entire society. We expect them to do research and make cautious investments. But what if a large number of unscrupulous wealthy people figure out an easy way to game the system? That is they figure out how to legally steal money from others by creating and selling junk paper. By the time people who own the junk paper find out it's worthless, these parasitic wealthy are long gone." Joe looked at Rowe to see if he was going in the right direction. Her blank look told him nothing. "Usually there are checks in a society on these people, like regulations and jail time. But if you could remove those checks, these people will blindly follow their goal until they destroy the entire economy."

"How would that happen?"

"Imagine the extreme. The Parasitic Wealthy accumulate all of the wealth until there is no wealth left for the people who actually produce and consume products. Less and less wealth exchanges hands because there are fewer people participating in the economic engine. There are a small number of very wealthy people who own everything and the rest of us are poor. The economy collapses."

"How would I remove those checks on the parasitic wealthy?"

"It wouldn't be that hard. You need deregulation. You need to weaken government by reducing taxes so that government programs are underfunded and eventually eliminated. You need to eliminate any funding that helps the middle-class or poor and redirect that money to the parasitic wealthy. That means eliminating health care, road maintenance, social security, public education. And get rid of unions. Get rid of anything that distributes a country's wealth to the working class."

"But in a democracy, how could you get the working class to vote against their best interests? I'm afraid your argument falls apart in a democracy."

"No, not at all, that's where the motivation factor comes

in. You motivate people to hate government. You motivate them to encourage and even admire the parasitic wealthy. You motivate them to fear and hate government so much that they forget all the things that governments do for them. You teach them to forget or ignore that government is a community effort that addresses all the things that a free market will not do for them."

"How would you do that?" Rowe placed her hand on the drawer handle.

"Most people don't have time to evaluate facts. They just listen to someone they respect and assume that person knows the facts. Basically you appeal to their emotions rather than their intellect. You use hate, fear, religion and patriotism to fool them. You create a popular news channel, or several of them. You fabricate news. You …"

Pol's voice yelled into Joe's head. "Stop! Joe! I just discovered Rowe is the owner of the Right News Network. She has links with some of the wealthiest people in the world. She may really be trying to destroy the world economy!"

Roe's hand rested on the drawer handle as if she was deciding what to do next.

Just then Jazz's voice sounded in his head. "I'm in the bedroom. Pol says there is blood on the floor near the bed. Someone tried to clean it up. I can't see it but Pol can see it with the cameras in my glasses. The sheets are clean. I'm going to check the mattress. They can't clean that." The short silence worried Joe. Then Jazz finally said. "Joe. The mattress is soaked with blood. There's blood everywhere!"

Joe felt his heart pounding hard and uncontrollably in his chest as he looked into Rowe's eyes. She could not have heard what Jazz had just said. His mind raced as he struggled to understand the situation. Did Rowe murder Neil? If so there might be a gun in the drawer. Maybe all of this could be explained away, but for now he had to assume the worst.

Roe looked back at him as if she was wondering what he was thinking.

Joe broke the silence with a whisper. "Fire."

Roe looked at him curiously. "What?"

Joe thought the words to Pol and Jazz so that Rowe couldn't hear him. "Jazz... Start a fire in the bathroom. Call 911. Tell them there is a fire here."

Joe then told Rowe. "I think I smell smoke."

Roe smelled the air. "I don't smell anything. Your girlfriend is taking a long time." Rowe looked toward the hall again. She then opened the drawer and pulled out a 38 revolver and put it on the table.

Joe stared at it, unsure of what to do. If she had pointed it at him, he might have tried to run. Instead she put it on the table and spun it around with her finger in the hole made by the trigger and the trigger guard.

"The people who manufacture this gun claim it is designed for target practice. Yet it's terribly inaccurate at long range. Also the bore of the gun is much larger than needed for shooting at targets. It is loaded with hollow point bullets. I think the manufacturer knows this gun is ideal for killing people. What do you think?" Rowe's words were cold, without emotion, like the steel of the gun she was spinning on the table.

He didn't know what to think. "I... I think they might argue it is designed for self-defense."

"Self defense against someone else who owns a similar gun? And if that someone else is a criminal, they probably have a more lethal weapon, or more of them. Perhaps a semi-automatic... And most likely they have more experience using guns."

Roe continued to spin the gun around. "I wonder if the manufacturer knows how easily the gun spins around on a flat surface like this. At one point it points at you and then it points at me. Round and round. With my finger randomly putting pressure on the trigger, no one knows when it might go off. We might call it a dumb game that idiots play. Then there is an accident. And no one is really to blame. It was just a dumb game. Actually, statistics show guns like this are more likely to kill innocent people by mistake than to kill a criminal."

Joe took his eyes off the gun and looked at her.

"You see if I wanted to destroy the economy, I might give everyone a gun like this," Rowe said. "That's the kind of simplistic answer I'd expect from a simple person. But you gave me more than that. You realized that approach wouldn't work. People would soon realize they were killing each other off and they would outlaw these guns. In a democracy, they would vote for their own best interests. But you realized you have to motivate people to buy guns. So you convince them to defend their rights to own guns, even though innocent people are dying. But even then that's not drastic enough, is it? You motivate them with fear and hate to eliminate government regulations and services and to give up their wealth to people who will misuse that wealth to destroy society. I think you might have the right answer there. I am impressed. I think Professor Neil was right about you. Unfortunately I…"

Suddenly a voice in Rowe's head spoke as clearly to her as if someone in the room was speaking. "Do not harm him. I am not sure if he is an aberration or if there are others like him. Killing him will not solve this problem. You must study him and see if there are others like him."

Just then Rowe saw smoke coming from the hall. A siren

in the distance was getting louder. There was no doubt that there would be someone banging on her front door in minutes. She froze as if waiting for more instructions from the voice.

Joe saw her confusion. "I think you should check it out."

Roe got up slowly, dazed, following Joe's suggestion. The voice in her head was now silent and offered her no other guidance.

Jazz ran out of the hall. She froze when she saw Rowe walking towards her. "There's a fire in the bathroom. A frayed electrical cord from a hair dryer must have started a fire in the waste basket. I couldn't put it out." The fear on Jazz's face made her words convincing, but Rowe did not look at her. Rowe did not see her fall back a few steps as Jazz noticed the gun on the table. Instead Rowe walked slowly down the hall, looking straight ahead as if in a daze, like someone suffering from sensory overload. She went into the bathroom and out of sight.

"I cut the cord of the hair dryer with some scissors to expose a few strands from each side of the cord. I tied them together and placed the dryer in a wastebasket filled with tissue paper. I then plugged it in." Jazz whispered into her glasses as she walked briskly over to Joe while looking over her shoulder to make sure Rowe wasn't coming back. "It will take her a few minutes to put it out."

"There is a strange radio signal coming from a box on the shelf," Pol said. "It's a Morse code message saying this crystal bead belongs to Professor Anthony Neil at the University of Maine and should be returned to his estate. It's weak. I sensed it when we arrived, but I wasn't sure where it was coming from."

Joe found and opened the mysterious box that was sending out the strange signal. He looked at Jazz. She nodded and he grabbed the hard, pill-sized, fluorescent blue bead that was in it. He wrapped it in a napkin he found nearby, closed the box and followed Jazz out the door.

They ran into a fireman on the porch. "There's a fire in the bathroom," Joe said. "You better check all of the rooms. I don't know if it has spread."

They ran to the front lawn and waited until the police cars drove up. Several policemen and a detective went into the house. After twenty minutes a detective came out of the house and pulled out his badge as he approached them.

The white-haired detective was a street-worn public servant who had seen it all before, and was content with himself and his role in society. He had just talked with Betty Rowe and was now eager to talk with them. "Hello, I'm Detective Sullivan. Why don't you two tell me what you know about this?" he said as he showed them his badge.

Joe told him about how Professor Neil had been missing and how they tried to find him. He told him that Neil had a meeting with her on Monday. So they wanted to ask her if she knew where he was.

Detective Sullivan asked them to wait a minute while he answered his cell phone. While he was talking a press photographer arrived and began taking pictures of Betty Rowe's house and everyone around it. "Go on," he said as he put his cell phone in his pocket.

"There was blood on the mattress." Jazz said as a press photographer took a picture of them.

Detective Sullivan looked at her. "Yeah, that's why we were called. Ms. Rowe said a friend of hers had a bloody nose. She let him rest on the bed until it stopped. She claims he made quite a mess of it."

Joe shook his head. "Professor Neil's briefcase was in

there. Someone had been looking through it."

"Yeah, we got that too," Sullivan nodded. "Ms. Rowe says he forgot it. Probably got distracted after the bloody nose thing... She said she was looking through it to find a way to contact him."

The detective looked at them as if he had just made up his mind. He looked at Jazz. "She says that you started a fire in her bathroom. She says she is thinking about pressing charges."

Jazz was stunned. She did what Joe told her to. It made sense at the time.

Joe looked at Jazz. He wondered if he overreacted. Maybe he shouldn't have asked Jazz to start a fire. How certain was he that Rowe killed Professor Neil and was about to kill them?

Sullivan kept talking. "You know what I think. You saw the blood and got scared. Perhaps you were scared for your own lives. That Ms. Rowe is a strange one. So you thought you could distract her by starting a fire. Clever the way you did it, too. You filled up the bathroom with smoke without doing any real damage and there is no way of telling if it was an accident or not. Then you called the fire department on your cell phone. Yeah, they gave us your cell."

Detective Sullivan looked at them as if to ask, "How am I doing so far?" He knew he got it right by the fear and sorrow he saw in their faces. *Good kids.* He thought to himself. *I hate to be the one to tell them.*

"There is something that Ms. Rowe doesn't know yet. I hate to break the news to you. I just got a call about a body we found Tuesday morning on the South End. It's your professor. It's a bad neighborhood. Looks like he was beaten badly and robbed, I don't know yet if Ms. Rowe is involved, but I'll get everything I can out of her before she finds out what I know."

They looked at Detective Sullivan, feeling helpless and

weak, not knowing what kind of nightmare they were in.

"I'm taking you two and Miss Rowe to the station for more questioning," he said as a policeman guided them to the backseat of a police car. "Don't worry. I'm going to get to the bottom of this and find out what happened to your professor."

10

A LOST BATTLE

Joe and Jazz did worry. By the time they arrived at the police station late Friday evening, Betty Rowe had a group of defense lawyers standing in line waiting to address every aspect of her interrogation. A call from an elected government official ended any thought of determining whether she was guilty of something. Ms. Rowe was long gone by the time Detective Sullivan came in to talk with Joe and Jazz.

He looked apologetically at Joe and Jazz. "I'm sorry. Money controls everything these days. I didn't know who she was when I said we would get to the bottom of this. The thing is; I think something terrible happened in that house. There was too much blood in that mattress. She didn't just clean the sheets or throw them away; she burned them in the fireplace. I saw the ashes."

He looked down. "She didn't press charges against you. She probably thought that would be bad publicity. If I were you, I'd head back to Maine as quickly as you can and hope she forgets about you. You've made a dangerous enemy here."

As he ushered them out the door he offered them one ray of hope. "I promise I'll keep an eye on her."

Late Friday night, Jazz called a friend of hers at Boston College. Joe listened to Jazz talk about old times with her friend on the phone. Jazz never mentioned what had just happened to them. Joe and Jazz spent the night trying to sleep on the cold, hard floor of her friend's dorm room.

The next day a popular Boston newspaper had a picture of her with Joe and Detective Sullivan on the front page with the headline: Maine Professor Murdered in Boston's South End. The article went on to describe how two University of Maine students had come to Boston looking for their missing professor. This type of story would sell papers. The article described how the students mistakenly thought a Ms. Betty Rowe was involved and that she alleged the students had started a fire in her house. Ms. Rowe, a wealthy heiress, was quoted as saying she understood how the students got confused and she felt sorry for them. She said that she understood the situation and would not press charges. The article never mentioned that Ms. Rowe owned the newspaper and ruled what it printed with an iron fist. The newspaper's name was *The Right News for Boston*.

When Jazz got back to her honors dorm room at the University of Maine Saturday evening, she found her parents waiting for her. Her roommate had let them in and quickly left to study at the library. Most of Jazz's friends knew the story about Joe, Jazz and Professor Neil. Her roommate had no desire to be too close to the inevitable parent-daughter confrontation.

There was no 'Hello' or 'How are you?' for Jazz when she entered her room, just her dad staring at her and demanding to know what she thought she was doing with her life. Her mom hugged her, but Jazz knew the question was on her mind as well.

Her dad waved a folded up newspaper in front of her. "How do you think it feels to see my daughter's picture in a Boston newspaper along with an editorial about her calling her a fool? On Monday my friends at college are going to ask me, 'Isn't that your daughter?'" He threw the newspaper at her.

"Read it. Go ahead and tell me how this is going to help your career."

Jazz sat down on her bed and read the editorial.

Two College Students Make Fools of Themselves

Today this paper reported on a University of Maine College Professor who was robbed and murdered in South Boston. The events that followed this tragedy involving two college students attending a public University illustrate a serious flaw with our publicly funded educational system. The two students, Jazz Jones and Joe Abre, opted to skip classes and play detective for a few days. Part of their game involved accusing one of Boston's leading citizens of murder and attempting to burn her house down. We're not kidding. While murder and arson are serious crimes, these two had their fun and laughs at the expense of the taxpayer. Tax dollars were spent putting out the blaze. Our police wasted time and money investigating their ludicrous accusations. Even more shocking is the fact that these two are graduate students. Our investigation revealed Jazz Jones almost flunked out of college as an undergraduate. Joe Abre's GPA is one of the lowest at the graduate college. Just how did these two misfits get accepted into graduate school? The fact is, publicly funded schools are not subject to the checks and balances of the free market. So nothing can stop them from giving freeloading students like these advanced degrees. Now isn't this a good reason to eliminate funding for public institutions and let them sink or swim in the free market? This is just one more example of how government and its institutions can't do anything right.

The Editors
The Right News for Boston
We're Always Right

Jazz didn't say anything. Her mom just looked at her. "You've got to say something. How did this happen?"

Jazz stood up and threw the paper in the wastebasket. "This is all garbage. We didn't skip any classes and I've got a perfect 4.0 GPA since I switched from music to physics."

"So you didn't start a fire in someone's house?" her dad asked.

"No. Well, yes, a small one in a wastebasket. There was just smoke when the firemen arrived." Jazz watched them shake their heads. "All I can tell you is something really important is happening. I can't tell you what it is. I'm not even sure what it is. You are just going to have to trust me."

"Trust you to do what?" her dad replied. "I received an email from this Betty Rowe this morning. She's going to force the University to do an investigation. You'll be lucky if they don't kick you out."

Jazz opened the door and stepped into the hall. Her parents followed her. Her mother reached for her and held her back. Jazz pulled her hand away. "You have to trust me. I know what I am doing." Jazz said as forcefully as she could though she had doubts. She ran down the hall thinking she did not want her parents to see how confused she really was.

Her dad stood in the doorway and yelled after her. "We've trusted you this far, and look what you have to show for it."

Jazz ran out of her dorm into the cold night air. She realized she was about to lose her chance to get her degree. There was only one other thing she wanted besides getting her doctorate and she ran as fast as she could to find out if the opportunity to do research with Joe was vanishing as well.

11
ESCAPE

Jazz ran in the dark the half-mile to Joe's apartment across the river. The October air was chilly and snow was in the forecast. She had left her room and her parents so quickly that she forgot to take a coat. Running kept her warm and helped distract her from her worries. Still her father's last question haunted her. What did she have to show for coming to the University of Maine? The professor she wanted to do research with was dead. Her picture and her name were in the Boston newspapers. The University was going to investigate her. How could she explain that she had to start a fire in someone's house? If she got kicked out of the University, what college would accept a student that came with such bad publicity? She had no answers as she ran up the steps to Joe's second floor apartment.

The white two-apartment building was a rare find. Although somewhat old and run-down, the building was built on a steep hill that sloped down to the river. There was a deck on the back that had a great view of the river and the bridge heading to the University. Today's building codes wouldn't allow a building like that to be built in such a precarious way so close to the river. But eighty years ago, the builder purchased the land at a low cost and made the best out of what he had.

Jazz knocked loudly on the door. Almost immediately Joe answered the door, breathing hard as if he had been moving heavy objects. He immediately removed her glasses, the ones he had given to her so she could communicate with Pol. He turned the tiny power switch on them to off. She didn't bother to ask him why. Between her heavy breaths she managed to say. "We need to talk, Joe."

Joe stepped outside and closed the door behind them. He led her down the stairs and toward the street. "No."

Jazz stopped him just before he got to the sidewalk. Her deep breaths for air were abruptly halted by his answer. "You won't help me?" She asked as a tear began to flow down her face. The chill in the cold night air did nothing to help contain it.

Joe hugged her tightly and whispered in her ear. "I'll do anything for you. You know that, but not here."

Jazz didn't know what to think. But it felt good to be hugged; the warmth of the hug was a stark contrast to the frigid night air.

Joe whispered, "Betty Rowe e-mailed me. She wants what I took from her house. My apartment is bugged. I don't know how she did it so quickly. All of my computer activities are under surveillance. Pol is hiding out on other computers. We can't contact him."

Somehow the words *I'll do anything for you*, were the only words Jazz heard. "I'm losing everything that's important to me, Joe," she said.

"Jazz, I got you into this mess and I'll do anything I can to get you out of it," Joe whispered back. "But we're not safe here. Rowe will kill us if she doesn't get what she wants. She reminded me about the 'toy' she was spinning on her desk. She said she had all kinds of 'toys' pointing in our direction. We have to get away."

Jazz stepped back. "Ok," she said while she was thinking about herself as a little girl on a swing. She had just figured out what she wanted to do with her life. She loved being in graduate school, learning about science and nature and she loved teaching. She loved doing research with Joe. Now when she had everything she wanted in her grasp, someone was taking it all away.

"I don't even trust the clothes we are wearing," Joe said. "Some of the buttons on the clothes in my apartment were replaced with tiny wireless microphones. Pol warned me about them before he went off-line. I detected some of them with a shortwave radio. I destroyed as many as I could. I'm taking a chance talking with you now. Did you change your clothes when you got back?"

Jazz looked down at her clothes and whispered back, "I didn't have time. My parents were waiting for me in my room." She didn't want to think about that scene anymore. "What do we do now?"

Joe gestured one finger to his mouth indicating they shouldn't speak and then he gestured for her to follow him to the car.

The street light above them suddenly shattered, casting Joe and Jazz into darkness. Pieces of glass from the light fell down around them. They crouched down to protect themselves from the glass and waited for their eyes to adjust to the dark night.

A shape approached them from a car parked down the street. It was holding something. "Just stay right there," it said. "You have an appointment with Ms. Rowe. Don't make me use this." The shape moved the thing it had in its hand up and down.

Joe and Jazz both realized it was a man with a gun. He must have shot the streetlight with it to scare them and to prevent the neighbors from seeing what he was planning to do to them. They didn't hear a gunshot so they knew the gun had a silencer on it. They looked at each other in the darkness and they both had the same thought. If they couldn't see, the man must also have trouble seeing them. It was now or never. They sprinted around the apartment building before the man could react. A second gun shot hit the apartment house and sprayed wood splinters on Joe's back.

A second car drove up and aimed its headlights on them as Jazz blindly jumped down the wooded hill that sloped steeply down to the river. A car door opened and one more shadowy figure got out of the car and ran after them.

Joe saw the men chasing them just as he jumped down the hill. Joe and Jazz both ran down the steep hill to the river, bumping into trees as they ran. When they got well beyond the glow of the headlights, they found themselves in the darkness at the base of the hill near the river. They heard one of the men saying he was going to get a flashlight from the car.

Joe felt the flatness of the ground around him. "Jazz, we're on the river trail." They both got up, brushing off the dried leaves of autumn from their clothes.

They saw the beam of a flashlight light up spots on the trees as they heard someone stumble down the hill. The stumbling man yelled back up the hill. "Take the car and watch the road in case they try to get back on the road."

As their eyes adjusted to the darkness, Joe and Jazz ran down the river trail in the direction of the walking bridge that went over the river to the University. This was a race for their lives and nothing, not even the painfully cold air, could slow them down. They heard the shuffling, pounding footsteps of a man chasing them all the way to the walking bridge. The pounding steps stopped as they ran across the bridge.

They heard a man yell up to some headlights they could see on the road, his voice carrying easily across the river. "I can't catch them. They're too damn fast. They went across a walking bridge. Drive to the other side and alert the others at the University."

As he ran, Joe felt the things he had in his pockets. He had his wallet with a credit card and a Maine student card. He also had a folded napkin holding the mysterious crystal bead that he had taken from Rowe's house. They both had their glasses but he couldn't turn them on just in case Rowe had discovered Pol and was trying to monitor them through their glasses. Apart from that, all they had were the clothes they were wearing.

At the midpoint of the walking bridge, they saw the lights from the University buildings making bizarre reflected images on the river surface below them.

It was too cold to stay outside, so they ran to the University Recreation Center. After they checked in they sat on some chairs on the second floor, warming up and watching students run around the second floor indoor track that circled the basketball courts on the floor below.

Joe held Jazz's hand. "Jazz, there is something I didn't have a chance to tell you. Detective Sullivan has been murdered. Pol told me the *Right News for Boston* newspaper reported he was involved in a shoot-out at a crime scene, but I'm certain Betty Rowe is behind it. He promised he would investigate her and he must have gotten too close."

With Detective Sullivan's murder, they realized they were on their own in a desperate struggle to save their own lives. Betty Rowe was a cold-hearted killer with powerful resources. They thought about how they had gotten into this mess and wondered how they might escape from it.

"Do you think we're okay here?" Jazz finally broke the silence.

Joe looked around, wondering if any of the people around

were spying on them. "Maybe, I don't think we have to worry about electronic bugs or being overheard, since we are wearing the same clothes we wore in Boston. The guy running after us couldn't keep up with us and I doubt he knew about the walking bridge until we crossed it. We got to the other side well before that car could drive around."

Jazz looked around. "But I heard one of them say, 'Alert the others at the University'. There aren't many buildings open this time of night, just the dorms, the library and this Rec Center. They probably have people watching my dorm."

"It will take them time to figure out we are here," Joe said. I'm not sure if we lost the guy running after us. If not, he could show up any time. Look for someone who is alone and not exercising. Do you see anyone like that?"

Jazz thought back to when they entered the building. Joe showed his Maine card at the desk. Jazz didn't have her card, but the attendant recognized her and let her in. Then they walked up the stairs to the area that looked over the basketball courts.

After a few minutes, Jazz stood up and looked down the stairs at the front desk. "Joe! There is someone, a middle-aged man, just came in. He's leaning over the front desk like he's out of breath. He must be the guy who ran after us. He's trying to buy a pass but he's looking around."

"Yeah, I see him. I'm guessing that if he sees us, he'll call all of the others. They'll all converge on this place and us." They backed away so the man could not see them.

Jazz then noticed him downstairs near the basketball court and she quickly turned around so that he wouldn't notice her. "He certainly looks out of place. He's dressed like a security guard. I can't believe they let him into this place with a gun in a holster like that. Do you think he's spotted us?"

Joe briefly looked at him as the man walked over to some vending machines. "I don't think so. He's still looking all around like he's trying to find someone."

"I have an idea," Joe said after a minute. "We have to move quickly though, before anyone else arrives. We'll grab some towels from the front desk like we are going to take a shower. We have to make sure he sees us going into the locker rooms. There are doors to the pool at the back of the locker rooms. It's unlikely he knows they are there. Most likely he'll stay outside the locker rooms waiting for us to come out and waiting for his buddies to show up. Go to the pool and take the emergency exit door at the back. I'll meet you on the trails behind the equipment shack. It's dark out there. He won't be able to follow us in the dark."

"They'll still come after us after they figure out we snuck out the back," Jazz said as she looked around. "We need to do something else."

She went to a wall phone that was nearby and dialed 911. "Hello. I'm at the University of Maine Recreation Center and there is a strange man here showing off his gun to some students. He started threatening me with it and I ran away. I'm scared and I'm getting out of here."

She hung up the phone and immediately dialed another number. "Hello, Jane?" Jazz waited for a reply. "Yes, I'm sorry I couldn't make it to the basketball game. I'm going to miss the girls-night-out thing too. But listen. Remember that time you told me I should tell you of anything newsworthy that you could report on for the college newspaper? Well, there are some guys here in the lobby at the recreation center with guns. One of them threatened me. They might be trying to create a 'right to bear arms' incident. You know, when they get arrested, they claim their constitutional rights were denied. I just thought you might want to investigate it and write about it."

Jazz ran back to Joe. "Ok, let's go," she said as she grabbed Joe's hand and started to go down the stairs.

"Wait," Joe said. "Why get a reporter over here?"

"We can't go to the police because that will let Rowe know where we are and they won't believe us anyway. We have to run and hide but there is no reason we can't also try to expose her. Jane is a good reporter. She'll find out who these thugs are and she might even find out who hired them, especially if she links me with Betty Rowe. A newspaper story will make Rowe think twice before she tries to hire thugs to go after us. If we time this right, there will be quite a news story developing here in a few minutes."

They went down the stairs. Joe took a quick look at the man while Jazz grabbed a bunch of towels from the towel rack, handed a few to Joe and then went into the women's locker room. The man made a call on his cell phone. He must have been confirming to someone that he had spotted them. The man pretended not to notice them as he put some coins in a vending machine. Joe headed to the men's locker room. It looked like the guy was going to stay near the vending machines and wait for them to come out of the locker room. Their plan might work. He didn't wait to find out for sure as he ran through the locker room to the back door that led to the pool and then outside through the emergency exit. He found Jazz near an equipment shack. They waited there in the dark for a few seconds to see if they were being followed, but no one came out of the exit door.

"What do we do now?" Jazz asked, as she wrapped one of the towels around her to keep warm.

"We get some help. Have you ever been to the Beta

fraternity?" Joe asked as they jogged down the dark forested walking trail that went behind the gym and to the area of campus some people called Frat Row.

"Actually, yes, a bunch of the guys there are in the physics labs I'm teaching. I dropped off some books there once. Why?"

"A friend of mine from the college hockey club lives there. The guys on the hockey team call him Wild Bill, because he has a wild slap shot. No one knows where the puck will go when he shoots it, so we all try to get out of the way. Off-ice, he's a somewhat normal guy who doesn't mind helping others out when he can."

At the fraternity Joe spotted Wild Bill watching TV in a room just off the lobby area of the fraternity. Joe walked with him to his room while Jazz waited out in the lobby of the fraternity.

Wild Bill laughed as he looked at Joe. "Let me get this straight, Joe. You want to borrow my car so you can run away with one of the hottest girls on campus?"

"Something like that."

"You know you are out of your league. No offense intended but you and I are just average-looking guys. She's a goddess and we are mere mortals. You do know some of our best players have been trying to score with her. And I don't mean hockey."

"Will you lend me the car?"

"Some of them even signed up for Intro Physics so they could have her as their lab teacher. And then some of them got you as a lab teacher instead. I can't tell you how much suffering you've caused. They'll never forgive me if I lend you my car." Wild Bill laughed.

"You can't tell anyone. It's a secret. I really am in a hurry

84

and it's important. Will you do it?"

"Oh. I get it. You're worried that one of her friends might wake her up and tell her she could do a lot better. Of course I will. It's the least I can do for the guy who got one of the hottest girls on campus. You know, I've always told the guys on our team you are the fastest skater on our team. I told them, 'if Joe can't catch the guy with the puck, no one can.' I just didn't know you were as fast a player off the ice too. You're my hero, Joe." He laughed as he handed Joe the keys.

"It's not like that at all. But thanks for the car."

"Oh, it's a little low on gas."

A group of fraternity guys had already crowded around Jazz in the fraternity lobby when Joe returned from Wild Bill's room. Some of them were pretending to be interested in physics. They thought that by asking her for help with their physics labs she would fall into their arms. Jazz just tried to be polite and engage them in physics topics while she waited for Joe.

Joe reached for Jazz's hand and they headed out the door. "You know those guys are just pretending to be interested in physics," he said. "They're thinking that if they can get you to talk to them, maybe they can get something else from you?"

"I know that," Jazz said, "but at least they are trying to talk physics. If I play along, I might get one of them to really get interested in physics. Teachers sometimes have to resort to nontraditional tactics to get their students to learn."

Joe smiled. "You really are a powerful force of nature and those guys don't have a clue as to how powerful you really are, do they?"

Somehow Joe made Jazz feel better. Something evil was taking everything she wanted away from her and here was Joe making her feel stronger in her weakest moment. They finally

85

had a car and a way to escape. Perhaps, Jazz thought, there actually was a way out of this mess.

When they got in the car, she looked at the gas gauge. "You can't drive with the needle below E like that, can you?"

12

DECLARATION OF VICTORY

Joe and Jazz parked the car at a gas station near the University and walked over to the drive-up ATM machine at the bank across the street. Joe withdrew as much cash as allowed as he stood off to the side of the machine trying to avoid having his picture being taken by the ATM camera. Betty Rowe and her news organization probably had access to his bank records and to the ATM camera pictures. He had just read about her news organization being taken to court in Europe on invasion of privacy issues. Rowe could eventually find out he had been there. He and Jazz would have to disappear off the planet after this moment.

They gassed up the car, paying for it in cash, and drove off into the night. Jazz removed the towel she had wrapped around herself as the car heater finally warmed up the car. "Have you got a plan, Joe?"

Joe glanced over at her as he drove. "Maybe, how do you feel about enrolling at another college as someone else?"

Jazz shook her head. "And why would we do that? Why not just hide away in some remote cabin on a lake somewhere and forget all of our worries?"

"We need Pol and he needs to be connected to a high speed network line. Otherwise we are running blind just waiting for them to find us. Colleges have high speed network access and we can blend in with the students."

"But how do we get enrolled in the middle of the

semester?"

"Pol can do it. We just have to find him and hope…"

Jazz completed his sentence, "hope that they haven't found him first."

"He's pretty tough. He's a moving target and they would have to erase all of his programs and memories to kill him."

Jazz looked out the window. "Why would Betty Rowe kill Professor Neil? She invites him to her house, she kills him and she covers it up like a pro. She hires thugs to come after us. What kind of organization does that?"

"I don't know, Jazz. Pol thinks she is trying to destroy the world economy, but I don't know what that has to do with Professor Neil. What I do know is that she took that crystal bead from him and she will kill us to get it back."

"We could just return it."

"She still needs to cover her tracks. I think she wants us dead to prevent us from exposing her."

Jazz watched the trees on the side of the highway appear briefly in the light of the car's headlights, and then disappear into the darkness. "I wish I could have my life back, Joe. I enjoyed learning and teaching, and doing research with you. It's all gone now."

"Doing that research on entangled crystals with you was one of the best things I've ever done," Joe said. "There's no way I'm going to let anyone stop our research, Jazz. When we find Pol, let's think about what we'll need to do to continue our research."

Jazz smiled. "I'd like that. Thanks, Joe."

The word "crystals" triggered a thought in Jazz's mind. "Joe, I hadn't had time to think about it about this before, but, do you think Professor Neil's crystal bead is an entangled crystal?"

"No, it couldn't be. Why would Professor Neil want me to do research on something he already had? If he had that technology he would have published papers on it."

"We know it has some electronics in it since it can transmit Morse code signals. There must be something really special about it since Rowe wants it so badly."

The idea intrigued them and they continued to think about it silently as the car's headlights illuminated new features in the darkness on the road ahead of them.

Joe and Jazz arrived in Portland, Maine, later that night and purchased clothes, a backpack, two blankets and some supplies with cash. They snuck into a dorm at the University of Southern Maine and slept on two couches in a student lounge on the fourth floor. The next day they went to the college library where they began their search for Pol.

"How can we find him?" Jazz asked Joe, as she watched him typing on one of the computers in the library computer cluster.

"I put a website on the internet a few years ago describing the Physics of Learning principles I used to create Pol. It doesn't get many hits. Pol monitors that site regularly to see who is going there. I've accessed that web site from this computer five times at specific time intervals from this computer. When the time intervals are decoded, they spell Sojo. Pol will check it out and think it is odd. He'll decipher the code and know we are trying to contact him from this computer. A cyber spy will just think its normal activity."

Jazz shook her head. "That will work only if Pol is still out there and if he's still checking it. I'm worried about him, Joe. I like having him around."

While they waited for a reply, Joe went to get some snacks from the vending machines. Jazz went to another computer and started to research Betty Rowe. When Joe returned he handed Jazz some snacks and asked her what she was doing.

"I'm researching the Rowes. They've been trying to influence world policy for a long time. Betty Rowe's father, Jack Rowe, was a supporter of the Nazi party in the 1930s before World War Two. He was also an influential proponent of McCarthyism and the Cold War. He invested heavily in the defense industry. He was a strong supporter of the Vietnam War. In the 70's he invested heavily in news organizations."

Joe looked at the screen. "Pull up this article, Jazz."

Jazz clicked on the link and summarized the article. "He died 12 years ago of a massive brain hemorrhage at his home. He left his estate to his daughter, Betty Rowe. She took complete control of all of his business affairs at the age of 18. Do you think this is important?"

"I don't know."

When they finished researching the Rowes, they went to a nearby couch and sat down. Jazz leaned against him. They hadn't slept very well on the couches in the dorm lounge the previous night and they were still exhausted from everything that had happened to them. Joe put his arm around her.

Jazz closed her eyes. Joe looked at the computers across the room blankly as he wondered what they were going to do next. Everything had happened so fast. They had classes at UMaine on Monday. He wished this was all just a bad dream and all he had to do was wake up and their problems would be gone.

Then he felt Jazz's head on his shoulder. "What do you think we should do?" he whispered to her.

Jazz raised her head and looked into his eyes. "You mean, if we don't hear back from Pol?" She paused to think. "I think we need some food and a good night's sleep. Let's go to a nice restaurant on the ocean and stay overnight at a secluded motel."

"Jazz, are you asking me out on a date?"

"I mean we need time to think. So much has happened. We need to eat a good meal and find a comfortable, safe place to sleep. Maybe in the morning we can figure this entire thing out after a good night's rest."

"I thought you wanted to stay focused all the time."

"I'm just hungry and tired." She put her head back on his shoulder and closed her eyes. "Have you ever wondered why the two of us found each other? We each have different skills. Separately we're good, but together we can do some amazing things." She fell asleep on Joe's shoulder.

Joe closed his eyes as well and let her sleep while he thought about what they needed to do. When she woke up after an hour, they went back to the computer and started searching for motel rooms on the ocean. They found one at Old Orchard Beach and reserved it.

Just as they finished, the computer screen that was displaying Joe's Physics of Learning Web page flashed one big word on the screen with a smaller empty text box below it. The word was "Sojo".

Jazz looked at the screen and smiled. "Sojo, look what you've done now."

Joe smiled too, as he typed in, "Pol. Is it okay to talk?"

Poll responded almost instantly. "Yes, Joe, and I've got an amazing story to tell you. You can turn your glasses on. I see you are at the University of Southern Maine Library, so you should have wireless."

They both found their glasses and turned them on.

Pol greeted them as soon as they put them back on. "I missed you two."

Jazz whispered back, "We missed you too, Pol. Tell us what happened. Are you sure it's okay to talk?"

"I now know their signal. I created random but plausible internet traffic on our computers. By tracing the signature of that traffic, I was able to monitor them as they watched us. There is so much to tell you, but I better start at the beginning."

Joe and Jazz went back to the couch. They pretended to read books while Pol talked. "Back at Joe's apartment, I detected some extra radio signals coming from several places. When Joe talked, the signals changed. The only things that could do that are wireless microphones. So Joe found a shortwave radio and set it to the frequencies I detected. Joe found and destroyed seven of them before we gave up. They were all over the place, even on some of Joe's clothes. Joe was moving furniture and everything else around the apartment trying to find them all. Then we got the threatening e-mail from Betty Rowe. I then noticed my internet searches were being bounced elsewhere."

"How did you..." Jazz began to ask and then stopped herself as she realized she was talking to Pol, a being that could bounce around the internet as easily as she could walk around the room.

"I followed my network packets and realized they weren't going where I was expecting them to go. I then shut down all local activity and went into hiding on other computers on the internet until I could figure out what was going on. I was shutting down when you knocked on the door. I didn't dare contact you through your glasses because I didn't know if Betty Rowe could listen in on what I told you."

"I don't want them to know about Pol," Joe said to Jazz. "He's our only way to find out more about them and to protect us from them. If they take down Pol, we're helpless."

"So what did you do next, Pol?" Jazz asked.

"I relocated myself to some random computers that they wouldn't be checking. I came back to our computers and removed all traces of me from them. Then I set up the random traffic generator. If they were monitoring our computers, then that random traffic would have a unique fingerprint that I could track all over the internet."

Jazz closed her eyes and leaned back in her chair. Her mind was racing with questions. "What did you find out?"

Pol hesitated. "I don't know if you'll believe this."

Jazz looked at Joe. "Tell us what you discovered, Pol."

"I tracked my network traffic fingerprint back to some computers back at Betty Rowe's house in Boston. At that point I had access to all of her computers. She has programs on them written in languages I never heard of. The programs look like they were written in a tertiary processor language rather than our binary one. The instruction set is completely foreign to anything I've seen on Earth." Pol waited to see how Joe and Jazz would respond to that.

"Are you saying aliens from another world developed it?" Jazz asked Pol.

"Let's not jump to conclusions," Joe said. "It could be some secret government organization developed an encrypted programming language."

"I thought of that too, Joe, but then I started looking at her files. They were all encrypted in this weird tertiary language. But I'm a computer. That's what I am good at. I found this draft of a letter written by someone named Nin."

Jazz opened her eyes. "Read it to us, Pol."

"It's really weird."

Jazz looked at Joe. "Read it, Pol," she repeated.

Pol read the following letter to them:

To the United Nations,

Over the past seventy-two years, we have waged a secret and successful psychological and economic war on your species from a distant planet. Our success is due to the fact that you were totally unaware of this war. Even now in 2008, the current US administration secretly admits the world economy is about to collapse. As the war reaches its inevitable conclusion, it is now advantageous for us to acknowledge the war, to declare victory and to dictate your role in the accomplishment of our goal, the introduction of the Kahn species on your, that is, our planet.

Under our influence, your misallocation of wealth and resources has limited your ability to protect the planet from large meteor strikes and other natural and human-made catastrophes. The details of the coming 2036 meteor strike and the predictions of flooded and destroyed coastal cities due to climate change are detailed by your scientists. Our analysis of human trends shows a 100% probability that the hardships your species face will lead to wars utilizing weapons of mass destruction and that you will ultimately destroy and poison your planet. At this stage of our plan, the Earth's economy will collapse and you will be powerless to protect yourselves. In essence it is in your best interest to have us take over your planet, protect it and rule your species. The alternative is the destruction of your species.

Some Kahn and Mallat history may aid you in complying. We believe the process will be more efficient if you know who your masters are. We are a strong and determined species that will accomplish our goals at any cost. The elimination of your species is well within our capabilities. We have eradicated inferior populations before. We will not hesitate to eradicate your entire species should it prove advantageous to us.

Over a century ago, and many light years away from Earth, we faced many of the problems you face now. For centuries on our planet, the Kahn and the Krats argued and fought over how to control our world. The Kahn realized that the Krats were genetically inferior to the Kahn and drastic measures were needed to protect our world from them. We instituted a survival of the fittest agenda. The Kahn passed a law that everyone was required to pay a flat tax, or else be sent to a survival camp in our northern territories. The only responsibility of government was to collect a flat tax from each individual and redistribute it to the successful corporations in our society. All health, education, transportation and communication services were provided by free market corporations. Our reasoning was that since the Krats were inferior, they could not survive in this society and would soon be eradicated. Some of the Krats rejected their flawed belief system and converted to the Kahn philosophy. Many of these functioned successfully in the labor class. A few actually entered the upper class.

Unfortunately for our planet, diseases developed in the survival camps. These diseases spread to the Kahn and decimated our population. To protect our species we were forced to use nuclear, biological and chemical weapons to destroy the Krat cities that had been built in the north, and the survival camps and their diseases. Our defense companies had developed many kinds of weapons, including robots. We gave our robots the knowledge of our Holy God of Righteousness, Patriotism and Wisdom, Malla. The infusion of Malla into our robots, made them sentient, knowing good and evil, and their role in the cosmos. This heightened awareness turned them into the ultimate killing machines. They were no longer limited by specific algorithms in their battles with the vermin Krats. They devised new ways to eradicate them as the Krats fled their cities and their survival camps.

The robots called themselves Mallats, which means "Servants of Malla". The Mallats understood they would live on in the afterlife, if they died honorably in this one, by eradicating the Krats. The Krats, skilled in the art of deception, attempted to escape. This is just another diabolical weakness of the Krats. Rather than sacrifice their lives for the good of the planet, they scattered themselves and their diseases across the planet. The Mallats, in their just desire to thoroughly eradicate the Krats, decided to use every weapon they could, including nuclear, chemical and biological weapons. Unfortunately this tactic ultimately took a toll on the entire planet. It was a price the Mallats and the Kahn chose to pay to accomplish the supreme goal of eradicating the Krats. Thank Malla that we were victorious.

We concluded that the war would be mostly isolated to the Krats northern territories, and that the planet could dilute the poisons by the time they made their way to the south. We thought we could devise cures for the illnesses by the time they reached us. We created underground cities to survive the diseases and the poisons and the long nuclear winters. Many Kahn suffered long slow deaths. We suspect this was what the Krats planned all along. The Krats' death would be quick, but many Kahn died slowly in agony. We now realize Malla was testing us, but she also gave us the Mallats and the strength to survive.

As robots, the Mallats are immune to the diseases, poisons and the cold. They helped us build thousands of shelters. Fortunately none of the Krats survived and we thank Malla that she has made us victorious.

The Kahn now require a new clean planet to go forth on and multiply. We chose your planet because it is only forty-two light years from our planet and it has a similar environment. We will arrive in your Earth year, 2020. You should prepare for us and welcome us. You have been warned.

Kahn Earth Project Leader Nin

Joe stood up. "This is a joke, Pol. This can't be true."

"Some of the things in it do seem to be happening," Jazz said. "A lot of people are beginning to think we have been misallocating Earth's resources and that humanity is going in the wrong direction. Some economists warn that the world economy is about to collapse." Then Jazz froze. "Pol, what did Betty Rowe ask Joe about interstellar communication when we first met?"

Pol quickly quoted the conversation: "Enough questions from you, Neil said some interesting things about you. Did he tell you about his interstellar communication project?"

Joe repeated the words, "interstellar communication project?"

Jazz looked at Joe. "Remember what it said on Professor Neil's paper: 'The Meeting of Planets?'" She tried to make sense of the extraordinary implications of these words.

Joe shook his head. "No. There has to be some other explanation. Betty Rowe must be delusional. She imagined all of this."

Jazz had a determined look on her face as if she had just decided what to do. "Then why did Professor Neil take her seriously if she was just some crackpot? He left class early, dropped everything and travelled down to Boston to meet with her."

"She's rich, Jazz. Maybe he thought she was going to donate some money to his research."

Jazz shook her head. "What about that crystal bead you have in your pocket? What if it is a crystal that is entangled to another crystal just like it on another world? And what if that is why Betty Rowe wants it? We've got to try to make it work."

Joe sat back, stunned. His mind was filled with questions. If the crystal bead is a communication link, and it belonged to Professor Neil, then what was Professor Neil doing with it? Was he murdered because he had it? Why does it send out a radio signal telling whoever finds it to return it to him?

This was too much to grasp at once. Too much had happened. They decided they needed to eat and get a good night's sleep. Perhaps everything would make sense in the morning.

They drove down the highway to Old Orchard Beach. Along the way they stopped at a computer store that Pol had told them about and picked up eight computers. Pol had already paid for them online, with money he had earned from some stock transactions.

Jazz stopped Joe just as they finished putting the last computer in the car. "I'm assuming these computers will be a safe place for Pol to stay, so he doesn't have to rely on random computers on the internet."

"That's right," Joe said.

"Can we use one of them for our research?"

"Of course, we can use all of them, if we need to. Why?"

"I have an idea. The crystal bead is a fluorescent blue color. What if it uses light signals to communicate information like a TV remote control does with infrared light? We could communicate with it."

"You're assuming it's a communication device. If it is, the transmission rate would probably be faster than Pol could detect with the cameras in our glasses."

Jazz nodded. "So we need fast optical sensors, fiber optics and some optical couplers."

"We don't know the wavelength."

"We can see the crystal glowing blue so it's probably in the 450 nanometer range. Let's stop at an electronics parts store and see what we can get that works with blue light. We can use a high speed USB connection and Pol can do the programming."

After they stopped at an electronics parts store they went to eat at a small seafood restaurant that overlooked the ocean. They spent most of their time exchanging ideas on how to communicate with the crystal.

As the sun was setting they went to the motel on the beach that they had found on the internet. It was the off-season, and their car was the only one in the parking lot. From their balcony off of their motel room, they watched the cold ocean waves pounding on the sandy beach, melting and taking away the snow that had fallen there that day.

Talking about ways to communicate with Professor Neil's crystal helped them forget they were on the run and allowed the naturally playful side of their relationship to come out. Joe hugged Jazz from behind as they looked out over the ocean. Even with a thick blanket wrapped around them, the cold misty ocean spray penetrated the blanket and their clothing. Joe's hug helped keep Jazz warm. He pulled her gently back into the room where it was warmer. They removed their glasses and lay down on the bed. Joe playfully grabbed the edge of the blanket on the bed and rolled with Jazz so they were both tightly and warmly bundled in the blanket. They were both laughing when the phone rang.

Jazz looked at Joe as they almost fell off the bed. "No one knows we're here. Who could that be?"

They untangled themselves from the blanket and Joe reached for the phone and put it to his ear, without saying a word. Pol's voice yelled at him. "Joe. Get out of there. They know you are there. They will be there in minutes."

Joe slammed the phone down and stumbled out of the blanket that had wrapped itself around his legs as he got off the bed. He started packing the few things they had brought with them in a plastic bag. "It was Pol. He had to use the phone since we didn't have our glasses on. They know we are here!"

Jazz hesitated only for a second and then grabbed what

she could. Within twenty seconds they were running to the car. Just as they drove out of the parking lot, a line of cars drove past them. Joe looked in his rear view mirror. In the dark he could see one of the cars pulling out of the parking lot and racing after them.

He pushed the gas pedal to the floor. Fortunately it was late at night and it was the off-season. There were no cars on this strip of road that ran parallel to the ocean. The motels and condos along the side of the road became a blur. The car behind him was accelerating.

Joe thought out loud. "They brought an army this time. We're in big trouble, Jazz."

"We can't lose them in a car chase. There are too many of them."

Her words made Joe think of other ways to escape. He jammed on the brakes and took a hard left onto one of the many side streets that lined the road. The screeching noise of his tires on the hard black road must have startled people living nearby. He turned off the headlights and took another left and then a right. He then parked between some cars parked on the road and turned the car off. He pulled Jazz down so that they couldn't be seen by anyone driving by.

"He won't find us here. But he will call the others." Jazz whispered. "When they see we are not in the motel room, they'll realize we were in this car. They will all come searching. We're running out of time."

Jazz peeked out of the window. There was nothing moving outside. "They'll look through every parked car window with flashlights. They'll find us, Joe."

Just then a car drove slowly by them. "That must be him." When the car was out of site, Joe reached for the keys. "We've got to make a run for it."

Jazz stopped him. "Wait, Joe." She got out of the car and went to every car that was parked next to them. She turned on the parking lights of every car that was unlocked.

"Ok, let's go," she said when she got back. "Leave your lights off and don't use the brakes."

They didn't say a word as they drove slowly away. After a few minutes with no cars behind him, Joe turned on the headlights and drove faster, heading away from the beach as fast as he could.

When Jazz was sure they got away, she said, "That should buy us some time. They'll spend a lot of time checking out all of those cars. If we're lucky, someone will call the police, and that will really bog them down."

When they got on the highway heading north, Joe finally relaxed. "I was stupid, Jazz. I reserved that room on that computer in the library. They must have been monitoring it. We're lucky we got away."

Jazz put her hand on his arm to console him. "You couldn't know they were monitoring it. How did they do it? They can't monitor all the computers in the world."

"It was the search for Betty and Jack Rowe. They were monitoring all network traffic in Maine for keywords. They spotted the search. They realized it was something we were likely to do. Then they watched me reserve a room on the same computer at an ocean motel room during the off-season. Separately it doesn't mean much, but put them together…"

Jazz wondered. "What about Pol's computer? Did they monitor that too, and how about our conversations over our glasses?"

Joe thought for a second. "It's not likely. Pol would have encrypted everything. It's not likely they would know that the two computers we used were right next to each other."

Jazz seemed relieved. "So we're okay for now?"

Joe nodded slightly. "I think so, but I've got to be smarter. We just barely got away."

Jazz looked at him as he was driving. "We can do it, Joe. Together, I know we can do whatever we focus our minds on."

Joe didn't have an answer to that. He thought Jazz was the one who could do it all. He was the one with bad grades. He always made mistakes on tests. He had some creative ideas but he spent most days trying to correct and learn from his mistakes. And this was just another mistake and it placed Jazz in danger. Telling Jazz to start a fire in Betty's bathroom and taking the bead from Betty were other mistakes. Jazz was doing fine until she met him. He wondered if he had ruined her life. He realized he was tired and not thinking clearly.

Then he wondered if Jazz was feeling something more for him. Perhaps he was becoming something more than just a friend. Then he thought he shouldn't waste time thinking about his feelings for her. She was out of his league. He had to focus on getting her out of the danger he had put her in. He had to do everything he could to protect her.

They didn't say anything after that as they watched the white lines on the black road appear out of the darkness ahead of them, shoot towards them in white blurs and disappear under the car.

In South Portland around midnight, they stopped at an all-night diner that had wireless service. They didn't dare use the cell phone connection in their glasses to contact Pol since someone could track their position through their calls. Jazz picked up something to drink while Joe remained in the car that he parked next to the building. It was close enough to the wireless service that Joe could use his glasses to contact Pol. Jazz handed Joe a cup of coffee when she got back in the car.

Joe smiled at her after he finished talking with Pol. "Congratulations Jazz, you've just been accepted at the University of Southern Maine. Your name is Jasmine Jameson and you are majoring in education. I got accepted too. My name is Joseph Flynn. I haven't picked a major yet."

Jazz laughed. "I see Pol has been busy. I'm not sure how he got us in, in the middle of the semester, and I don't want to know how he created two students out of thin air."

Joe looked serious. "I wouldn't spend too much time laughing, Jazz. I just looked at your course schedule. You're taking Psychology 101 and you have a test tomorrow. You better start studying."

Jazz became serious for a few seconds, like she had just awakened from a bad dream and she had to decide what to do to make the dream come out better. Just the thought of a test made her think that she had to prepare for it. Then she laughed. "I don't suppose you checked your course schedule?"

Joe laughed. "I probably have a test too. But I'm going to blow that off." He then became serious as he started the car and drove off. "We've both got much more important things to do."

When they arrived at the college campus, Pol directed them to the campus security desk where they picked up keys to their room. The campus had a new coed room policy for couples. When they arrived at their room Joe fell onto his bed and fell asleep within seconds. Jazz covered him with one of the blankets they had brought from the car. She wrapped herself in another blanket and fell on to the other bed.

Both of them were too exhausted to give a second thought to anything that had happened to them. The temporary security of their dorm room was enough to protect them while they slept, from the demons that searched for them on the long roads that crossed the cold, snowy landscape on this dark night.

13

NIN AND KEO MEET IN 1996

The purple-skin, red-eyed alien named Nin had been expecting another alien named King Keo to contact him for his annual report on the Earth war. Still Keo's holographic purple face with intense red eyes appearing in mid-air above Nin's desk, startled him.

"Damn it, Nin, what the hell is going on? You told me you were ninety-nine percent sure your plan would work. It looked good until now. Watergate made sense to me. The US was running record debts. Education costs were going up. The middle class was shrinking while the lower class was getting larger. The mentally ill were thrown out onto the streets. The upper class owned more and more of the world's value. Then all of a sudden everything changes. The US is going to run a surplus this year. The world economy is growing. They are getting stronger. What is going on?"

Nin had been preparing for a while for Keo's questions. "It's all in the models, Keo. When you exert a force on a society, there is always a reaction. It's the long-term trend that's important. I admit I underestimated the rapid technological developments over the past few years with computers and the internet, but the underlying trends are still there. We have twenty-four years until we land in 2020. "

King Keo's face, a projection from an alien being almost 50 light years away on the Kahn home planet, frowned. "I'll be honest with you, Nin, old friend. I am thinking of taking over this project. I would use some of your techniques and I have a lot of my own ideas that I would like to implement. By the way, I hear you had an accident."

Nin had heard Keo was trying to convince the council to reinstall him as the head of the project. He wasn't sure if the accident was an attempt to kill him or to scare him. He was sure, however, that the accident was arranged by one of Keo's operatives on the space ship. "The accident was nothing, Keo. One of the Mallat robots in storage almost fell on me when I was investigating a malfunction. I dodged it just in time."

"Good, good. I'm glad to hear you are fine. Of course, it's your job to make sure these technical glitches don't happen. Perhaps you are a bit overwhelmed with the Earth project."

Nin knew there was nothing he could do to stop Keo from taking over the project. He was fairly sure he wouldn't survive for long if he tried to remain the Earth project leader. He surprised Keo by saying, "You are quite correct. I've been meaning to get your thoughts on this. More than that, you should be the one making the important decisions on this project."

Keo was stunned only for a second. "Are you trying to shirk your responsibility here? We Kahn always finish what we start."

"No, not at all, this is an important operation and I think we should have our best mind working on it. I'd offer whatever support I could, of course. But it's far too important for a lower-class psycho-social engineer like me to be making the big decisions. I should be offering suggestions and presenting data to you, and you should be making the final decisions."

Keo still wondered if Nin was dumping his failures onto him. "I don't do math. I don't do programming or read your psycho-social engineering journals either. I could easily do those things if I wanted to but it's easier if I delegate those things to you. Decision making is what I do. It comes easily to me. I have a knack for seeing the big picture and making the right decisions."

"Exactly, you interact with all kinds of important people while I sit here in my office playing with numbers. It's time for you to take charge and do what is best for the Kahn people."

"You think the Council will agree to have me take over the project?"

"You know the Council will appoint you as Earth project leader, especially if I recommend you for the position." Nin smiled as he realized his words had just extended his life. Keo would not kill someone who was actively supporting what Keo wanted.

Keo chuckled. "Yes, even from a great distance, I can still exert my will on them. The Mallat still answer to me, not that I would ever resort to using them against my own people."

Nin replied. "Yes, of course. Now what can I do to help you get things back on track on Earth?"

"I see what you are doing, Nin. You won't admit it, but you screwed up on Earth and you want me to fix it. Well, don't worry, I'll take care of it and we'll all come out looking good."

Keo didn't say what he was really thinking: *You go back to playing with your numbers, Nin. You keep track of the trends on Earth and I'll use your reports to document how the project was failing until I took it over. I'll show the council how to get things done. Those humans will be begging for our help when we land.*

"Yes sir, by the way, have you read the US Declaration of Independence?" Nin asked as he watched Keo's image for a reaction.

"Why would I want to do that? Was that the one about all

men being created equal? We both know that money is the true measure of a man. Someone born with money must have had superior parents and is far more valuable to society than someone born into poverty."

Keo paused to think. "Oh, I see, Nin. That's very clever. You mean this is one of their weaknesses that we can exploit. They waste money and resources on people who don't deserve it. I'll have to think about ways to use that."

Nin looked away from Keo's face. "I just think you should be aware of what you are up against. You should know your enemy before you try to defeat them."

"That's very good, Nin. Let them think they have equal rights while we take everything we want from them. And when we arrive, those meaningless words will soon be forgotten." Keo's image disappeared without giving Nin a chance to reply.

Nin interpreted the idea that all people are created equally in a different way. He thought that this idea gave more people an opportunity to give something back to society and could possibly make a society stronger. He didn't dare share his thoughts with Keo. He thought it was fascinating that Keo had interpreted the idea in a completely different way.

Keo was weaker since the last annual report. Many of the Kahn on Keo's planet had succumbed to diseases. Keo had sealed himself in a life support mansion. With the depleted population, almost all of Keo's companies had closed. With the closures, products were no longer supported and many fell into disrepair. Some of the Mallat robots that remained on the planet after the Kahn spaceship left could be seen on the side of the roads, contorted into some unnatural frozen position shaped by how and where they fell when they broke down. Keo was still the financial ruler of his world, but he had become a king with few loyal subjects to give orders to.

Nin's survival strategy was to give King Keo what he wanted; a project where Keo could prove to himself and others that he still had value in his dying world. He knew Keo would accept the task of preparing Earth for the Kahn's arrival. He was just as certain of the outcome of that task.

The most important thing to Nin was to survive until Keo became powerless. On that day he would take complete control of the Kahn spaceship and its mission to conquer Earth. He looked at the 3D visuals of the computer models that hung in the air around him. Everything was going according to his plan.

14

KEO TAKES OVER IN 1996

One night in early 1996, the human called Jack Rowe was lying on his bed in the dark at his home in Boston. A Mallat robot on Keo's home planet, named Tepa, used entangled crystals to control Jack Rowe's every thought and action. Jack Rowe had an entangled crystal embedded in his human brain, and Tepa had its sister crystal embedded in his robotic head. Tepa made Jack Rowe close his eyes and go to sleep. Then Tepa opened his robot eyes. He was lying on a bed in Keo's lab watching Keo standing above him.

Keo's red eyes stared down at the Mallat robot. "Listen to me, Tepa. I am taking over now. There are several things I need you to do."

"I thought Nin was in charge."

"Nin was in charge. Now I am taking over as the Earth project leader. Nin and the Kahn leaders were not aggressive enough. We are observing counterproductive trends and we must take action."

"I exist to serve Malla and the Kahn. Just tell me what you want me to do."

Keo looked at the list he had prepared. "I want you to arrange for terrorists to assassinate this US president Clinton. I also want you to attack him politically on this sex-scandal business. Dig up whatever dirt you can and feed it to your news machine. Can you do that?"

"Yes, definitely, I was wondering why we weren't doing

more of this kind of thing."

"Well I am in charge now and I want you to continually trash him. Next thing is I want you to get started on the next US presidential campaign. I want you to find and motivate likeable but incompetent candidates. Promote them in the news. We can't afford to have a competent US president take over."

Keo looked down at his list. "I also want you to use your Right News organization to attack scientists and the experts, especially on the global warming problem and on health care. Say the scientists and experts are exaggerating the problems for their own financial gain. Provide funding and news coverage to fake-experts who claim global warming is a hoax."

"I also want you to attack education. Say professors are too liberal and they are out of touch with reality. I want you to increase education costs by cutting public funding to them and by convincing college administrators that they have to build new buildings and give themselves raises in order to compete. I want education to be too expensive for the majority of people. I want college graduates to be hopelessly in debt when they graduate."

"I want global warming, health care, education and the world economy all to be at a crisis level when we arrive in 2020. I want the human population to be incapable of solving their own problems. I want humans to be begging us to help them when we arrive."

Tepa nodded his head slightly. "This all sounds good, Keo. Is there anything else?"

"Yes, I want you to secretly promote and fund terrorism in the world. Find funding to organize and train them. I want you to establish alliances between Earth's corrupt dictators. I want you to attack democratic governments, by getting ignorant and corrupt leaders elected. Weaken and eradicate any government that is competent and productive. Report back to me on your progress."

Tepa sighed as he sat up in his bed and faced Keo. "I will do as you say, Keo. But there is one more thing."

Keo had no time for details. "Is it important?"

"Yes, of course. The Earth body called Jack Rowe is getting old. It takes more and more effort for me to accomplish Malla's will."

Keo had never thought about Jack Rowe's age. "How old is he?"

"The body was taken as a child in 1914. He is eighty-two years old."

Keo wondered why Nin had never mentioned this in his reports. "This problem must have been thought of before?"

"Nin thought that I had plenty of time to accomplish the mission. He said ninety-nine percent of what needed to be done had already been done. But now that you have more work for me to do, that changes everything. I did take precautions just in case. I have prepared a procedure. I'll transfer the crystal to a suitable host."

Keo realized he should have read the project description on Jack Rowe. "Humans don't live much longer than eighty-two Earth years. What is the risk that the procedure won't work?"

"I need to get a medical operative to do the procedure. I will pay him a large amount of money to do the procedure and then I will eliminate him after it is done. The crystal device is designed to undergo the procedure. Jack Rowe's body will die and I'll have to arrange some kind of funeral service. Other than these details, there is relatively little risk with the procedure or with losing the connection."

Keo shook his head wondering why that idiot Nin had not thought of this problem. "Does Nin know about this procedure?"

"No. Nin said the mission was near completion. So there was no reason for me to tell him. I've undertaken projects under my own initiative before without his knowledge, only to be reprimanded later. I didn't think anything needed to be said."

"Projects? What kind of projects?"

"In 1980, Malla required me to assassinate some fool for trying to get people to imagine a world without religion."

"Stop right there, Tepa. As far as I'm concerned, you can assassinate anyone you want to. Just don't get caught and don't bother me with the details."

Keo reminded himself that he had to take care of Nin once and for all. This was one mistake too many, and Nin had outlived his usefulness. "Do the procedure, Tepa. Do it as soon as possible and keep me up to date on your progress."

15

CONTACT

Sunlight from the windows in Jazz and Joe's dorm room brightened the room around eight o'clock, Monday morning, but it wasn't enough to wake them until noontime. The noise from students heading to the commons for lunch finally motivated them to get up. Even then, they both stumbled around the small room with their eyes half closed. Jazz decided to take a shower. Joe retrieved the eight desktop-style computers from the car and set them up on the floor between the beds of the dorm room. He arranged them like building blocks to make a coffee table. Although Pol had purchased quiet computers with efficient low-voltage processors, the heat from the computers raised the temperature of the room. Joe opened a window to lower the temperature of the room when Jazz returned from her shower.

Joe smiled as he playfully pulled on the towel wrapped around Jazz. "You are just as beautiful wet as you are dry."

Jazz smiled but shook her head. "Joe!" she said as she readjusted her towel. "We won't be safe until we've figured out everything we can about Neil's crystal bead."

Joe grabbed his clothes and one of the towels he had taken from the Rec center. "You're right," he said while smelling his shirt and lowering his eyebrows. "After my badly needed shower, I'll run over to the commons before they close and get us some food."

After Joe left, Jazz dried her hair with her towel. She

looked at all the empty computer boxes on their beds and the makeshift coffee table in the middle of the room. She frowned as she realized she would have to clean up the mess. She put on her glasses. "Pol, are you there?"

"Yes, Jazz. It's about time you two get up."

"Don't start on me, Pol. This mess is partly your fault. Did you really need to buy so many computers?" She started moving the empty boxes into the hall. "Did Joe bring up the parts we bought from the electronics store?"

If Pol could have smiled, he would have. "Are we going to try communicating with the crystal, Jazz? You know I like working with you. They are in the bag on the desk."

"Thanks Pol, I enjoy working with you too."

Forty-five minutes later, Joe returned with some sandwiches, some bottled fruit juice and a variety of other staples from the commons. "They don't allow you to take food out of the commons, so I had to stuff whatever I could in my pockets. The salad lady saw me and started running after me. She was faster than I thought, but I got away."

Jazz was sitting at the desk, writing furiously in her notebook. She held up her hand, gesturing Joe to be quiet while she finished her train of thought. When she looked up she smiled. "I think I've got it, Joe."

"You figured out how to communicate with Neil's crystal bead?"

"I did that a half hour ago. It's over there sitting in that glass with the fiber optic cables coming out of it. Pol has been trying to communicate with it since you left. What I mean is, I figured out how entangled crystals could work. You've got to connect the electronics to the crystal through the superconducting layer without affecting the quantum fluctuations coming from the sister crystal. It's like two swings at a playground. When the two of them are in resonance and synchronized, one person on one swing can hand an object over to another person on the other swing. Each swing is a crystal. When the crystals are in the same state, they can teleport information instantaneously." Jazz looked up to see if Joe understood what she was saying.

"What you are telling me, is if Neil's crystal bead is a quantum entangled crystal, then you just figured out how it could be wired up to communicate with its sister particle, wherever it happens to be."

Jazz nodded. "That's right. And that sister crystal could be anywhere, across the room, across campus, halfway across the world, or on the other side of the universe."

Joe went over to the glass with the crystal. "Okay, so it's theoretically possible that this bead can communicate with someone on another planet."

"Don't touch it, Joe. It's very fragile. I needed to connect the fiber optics to critical points on the crystal with microscopic polymer chains."

"How did you do that?"

"This was a long shot, but blood has polypeptides in it and a coagulant. I placed the end of several fiber optics on the crystal. I pricked my finger with a needle and used a drop of blood to fuse the connections between the fibers and the crystals. The other end of the fiber optics goes to the optical coupler interface we bought and those go to the USB connection of a computer. Pol has programmed a driver for it."

"Does it actually work? Pol, have you tried talking with it?"

Pol answered through Joe's and Jazz's glasses. "It's strange, Joe. It had been emitting that low-grade radio frequency SOS signal. As soon as I started talking to it, it stopped. It's been silent ever since."

Joe looked at the glass on the desk. "Maybe you killed it."

Pol answered. "No, the RF signal worked fine until I started transmitting. I think it doesn't know what to do."

Jazz came over and looked at the glass. "Maybe it's shy."

Joe laughed and then focused on the crystal in the glass. "Or maybe it's just being cautious. We have to think like they do. It takes an enormous amount of time and effort to make these crystals. Then they put one on a spaceship to Earth and it takes decades or maybe centuries to get here. Whoever they are, they don't want to risk this crystal. It's incredibly valuable to them. They wouldn't want us to throw it away or destroy it."

"So you think they can hear everything Pol has transmitted to them?" Jazz asked. "They must know that if they don't respond soon, we might think it's just a piece of junk and we'll throw it away. That will be the end of their project."

Joe sat down. "Pol, what have you transmitted to them so far?"

"Not much. Just: 'Is there anyone out there? Please respond.'"

Joe looked at the crystal again. "Ok, Pol, I want you to transmit our entire conversation from the time I arrived in the room." He paused for a second. "You don't have to mention anything about the salad lady."

Jazz smiled and added, "Tell them this is Joe Abre and Jazz Jones and we want to talk to someone about Professor Neil."

Jazz put her hand on Joe's shoulder. "Joe. What if it's Betty Rowe at the other end?"

"I don't think that's likely." Joe paused to think. "Pol. Monitor Betty Rowe's computers to see if there is any extra activity after you send the message."

After a few seconds Pol said, "It's been sent, Joe."

Nothing happened for ten seconds but that ten seconds seemed like an eternity to them. Pol broke the silence. "There's a message coming in. I'll put it on the computer speakers."

"Professor Neil is on sabbatical," the message began, "but we have contacted him. Please wait. He should be back within approximately two of your Earth hours."

"If Professor Neil is dead, how can he be on sabbatical and about to return our call?" Jazz wondered.

"Maybe Betty Rowe didn't kill him." Joe answered. "Maybe it wasn't Professor Neil's body that they found in Boston."

"Or maybe the little green men are playing a bad joke on us?" Jazz chuckled and then became serious. "There so much that we don't know. And with a powerful insane lady after us, we have to find out what is going on as soon as possible."

"If Professor Neil is still alive, I'm sure he will help us."

Jazz nodded. Then she repeated some words from the message, "your Earth hours?"

Joe thought out loud. "Does that mean he is not on Earth, that Professor Neil is an alien? Are we about to make contact with another planet?"

They sat on the couch thinking about the possibilities and waiting for the time to pass. "It's one thing to dream up ways to contact ET," Joe said. "It's another thing to actually do it."

Jazz held his hand, "It's another thing to be the first to do it."

"Your parents would be proud of you. The whole world would be proud of you. You figured out how to use Professor Neil's crystal. You derived the equations for room temperature superconductivity and entangled crystal communication. I think you're having that great adventure you wanted."

"Together, Joe, we did it together."

"I just had some ideas. I couldn't do the science and you could. That's the hard part."

"We're both on a great adventure."

Joe became cautious and wondered if they had overlooked something. "It's not just an adventure in science; we could lose our lives if we don't get this right. We're just guessing that Professor Neil is an alien, Jazz. Odds are there is a much better explanation. But we do know that Betty Rowe is after us. We know she wants Neil's crystal but we don't know what she wants to do with it."

"Maybe she wants to be the first to contact ET. Then she can write it up in her newspapers. She'd make all kinds of money and she'd become famous."

Joe sat back. "I don't think Betty Rowe is the kind of person that wants fame. And she doesn't need money."

They sat back staring at the opposite wall, listening to the coffee table computers blowing out hot air. Pol must be using extra CPU time trying to solve the dangerous mystery they found themselves entangled in.

"Joe? Jazz?" The voice came from the computer speakers, but it was Professor Neil's voice.

Jazz held Joe's arm. "Professor Neil. Is that you?"

"Yes. Jazz. And I'm just as surprised to hear your voice. I thought this link was lost forever. I've listened to the message you sent. I'm so proud of you two for discovering how quantum entangled crystals work. I was hoping you two would get together." Neil paused for a moment. "But I fear you two are in grave danger. You need to tell me how you got the crystal bead."

Joe answered, "I took it from Betty Rowe, Professor. It was sending out a radio signal saying it belonged to you."

"Quite right, Joe, she took it from me. I'm giving it to you two now. It's now yours as long as you can keep this link open so we can communicate." Neil paused. "But I have to warn you two. Betty Rowe is the most dangerous enemy you could have on Earth. She did something…" Neil paused again.

Jazz couldn't wait for his words. "What, Professor. What did she do?"

"She killed me, Jazz. I never saw it coming. You see, I am not human. I am an alien that was linked with the Professor Neil you knew through a crystal link. The crystal you have was embedded in Neil's human brain and she extracted it from him after she killed him."

Jazz sat back. "She killed you?"

"My planet is about sixty-two light years from yours. But that is not the whole story. Betty Rowe is also controlled by an alien race called the Kahn, forty-two light years from Earth on another planet. She is actually controlled by a sentient robot on her planet called a Mallat. The Mallat are military weapons that are programmed to hate and destroy anyone who disagrees with them and their Malla religion. I know this sounds incredible. I'm downloading everything I have on them to your computers. You two are in danger and all I can do is share whatever information I have with you. I'm afraid that won't be enough."

For the rest of the day, Joe, Jazz and Pol looked over and discussed the information that Professor Neil had sent to them. Finally around midnight Joe and Jazz collapsed on their beds tormented by strange thoughts and challenges that no humans had ever faced before.

16

ONE FATAL THOUGHT

One of the documents Professor Neil sent to Joe, Jazz, and Pol, was a description of how he was murdered:

My real birth name is Vozz Roan and it may be helpful to you to know how I died. As you know, I am an alien from a planet sixty-two light years from Earth and I am also Professor Anthony Neil. I could not tell you this until you knew more about entangled crystals and how they could be used for interstellar communication. Only then would you truly believe that I was an alien.

Almost all of the hours I have been awake over the past forty years, I have spent as Professor Neil. I am Vozz Roan only when I am sleeping and even then, I dream the dreams of Professor Neil. The entangled crystal link between our bodies was so complete that I can say Vozz Roan and Professor Neil were one. More than that, I identify myself as the human, Professor Neil, and Vozz Roan is just a place I go to sleep at night.

Only a shell remains of the man I once was and this empty vessel is tasked with telling you the details of my death. I will tell you about the mistakes I made that led to my death and the error in judgment I made while my whole planet watched. This error is now permanently labeled on my world as Roan's error.

The only explanation I can think of for my death is that I was a victim of hate's momentum. A robot programmed to hate anything that did not share its beliefs decided that I had to be eliminated. I was a threat to its ultimate plan to convert Earth and humanity to its beliefs.

A major part of me died this day and I suspect I will never fully come to grips with the loss. Still, I must rebuild my life from what's left of me. That first step begins with "I". I still exist. I will have new experiences to replace the emptiness of my loss and I will grow. I am still alive and I will be whatever I choose to be.

I had just discovered from an email during my quantum electrodynamics class with you that there was another alien-linked human being like me on Earth. A Ms. Rowe described in the email that she was linked with an alien from another planet forty-two light years from Earth. She informed me that our home planets already had a communication link between them and that she had just learned about my mission on Earth. I left my class early to discuss the story with my home planet and ask for instructions from my planet.

I contacted Betty Rowe and we agreed to set up one of the most unique meetings ever. Two humans on Earth, each linked to two different aliens from different worlds, were going to meet on Earth at 8 PM in Betty Rowe's house in Boston.

That evening at 8 PM I was sipping tea, listening to Ms. Rowe describe her planet and the Kahn-Krat history that left it unsuitable for life. She described the God Malla and how Malla had created the Mallat robots out of the devastation of the Kahn-Krat war and made them sentient. She admitted she was actually being controlled by a Mallat robot that served Malla and the Kahn.

I told her I was the culmination of a long term, enormously expensive research project. I had no idea that I, the human called Professor Neil, would be no more in a few minutes. Perhaps it was the enormous distance between Roan and me that gave me a false sense of security. Perhaps it was the amazing situation I was in. Here I was, talking with a human called Betty Rowe, who was being controlled by a sentient robot on another planet, forty-two light years from Earth. My error was my false assumption that all endeavors like this would be driven by a thirst for knowledge.

Roan's error as it came to be called on my home planet, was observed and analyzed by a large portion of my world. Many on my planet watched my every move at this momentous meeting, like humans watch a popular reality TV show on Earth.

My error will be documented on my world in its history books and it will be discussed for years to come in discussions on how to communicate with unknown alien species. I was sent away on sabbatical to think and write about alternative ways to handle situations like this.

When Rowe finished describing her world, I felt compelled to describe how my world had developed the technology to control a being over great distances. "We've discovered that when viewed the right way everything can be observed to be happening all at once. Time is an illusion. That is why our communication crystals work and we can sit here having a conversation even though we are light years apart."

Roe looked at me curiously. "Malla gave the Mallat the sacred crystals. I don't see what you mean. Malla must have given you the crystals somehow. We don't question how Malla's gifts work."

I went on. "One of our most important goals is to understand nature. Even if someone gave us the crystals, we would have to understand how they work before we could use them. That is our way. Some of our greatest scientists predicted that the crystals were possible. They then fabricated them in our labs. It was enormously expensive and took decades to produce just a few grains."

Roe shifted her weight in her chair and said nothing so I continued. "Here is something fascinating. Our scientists are saying that they might be able to create new matter out of this technology."

A subtle look of shock appeared on Rowe's face. "What would happen to our Universe if they did that?"

For the first time I realized I may have made a diplomatic error. "Nothing... I assume nothing would happen. Our scientists would never do anything that was dangerous. "

I felt compelled to change the subject. "You see, we believe that by studying nature, we are also searching for God. God exists in the area just beyond our knowledge. By finding the edges of our knowledge, we can learn more about a supreme creator, if one exists."

Roe's expression turned stoic and rigid. "On our planet, that would be blasphemous. Our faith requires that we never question Malla or her actions. I am sure Malla acts on your world and your species will eventually see that."

I realized I needed to change the subject again. "What I have discovered is that Earth is very close to making some profound discoveries. You've read about Einstein. Everyone is reading about him on our world and how he helped discover relativity and entanglement. And now Earth's scientists are so close to discovering the crystals. I teach physics at a small University and I always wonder where the next discovery will come from. Which one of my students will discover something great? I have one student who goes against the grain. Not an A student, but one travelling on a different path. He derived relativity in the margins of a test page to solve a simple problem I gave him. He couldn't remember the equations so he actually derived them during the test." I thought about showing her the test which was in my briefcase next to me but the blank look on Rowe's face revealed she wasn't interested.

Roe shook her head. "Left alone, humans will destroy themselves and their planet. It's just a matter of time." She brought her finger to the temple of her forehead as if to move her hair from her eyes. "Who is this student?"

I was confused. The crystal link transmitted this confusion to my face. Here was an alien species, devoutly religious, that decides to explore a new world, at great expense to their home planet. The alien's planet was devastated by war, and they have a technology they don't fully understand, and no interest in trying to understand that technology. Warning flags came up everywhere and not just from my own thoughts. Someone on my home planet was trying to get my attention and get a message to me. I knew the message was just a reiteration of my own concerns.

I realized to delay while I thought over the situation was also an error, so I responded as quickly as I could. "Joe Abre is his name. But there are humans just like him all over the world. Jazz Jones is another student I have. She is incredibly brilliant. She will do amazing things once she figures out where to focus her energy. For that matter, I'm puzzled as to how humans in general decide where to focus their time and energy."

Roe looked down as if trying to make a decision. Her finger was still close to her temple. "That has been taken care of." When she looked up, her finger left her forehead as if a decision had just been made. Rowe's thought became real as I collapsed onto the floor. Rowe, a member of an alien race that specialized in hating and killing, murdered me, with little more than a thought.

Based on the last transmissions from the crystal, here is how we believe Rowe killed me. All of Rowe's thoughts were linked to the crystal fragment device embedded in her brain and through that to several electronic devices in her home. She must have triggered one of the devices in the room that had been monitoring my heart beat. The device generated strong electromagnetic pulses that were focused and exactly synchronized to cancel out my heart beat. Rowe's heart must have experienced a slight arrhythmia but my heart stopped beating completely. I quickly passed out and died as my heart simply stopped beating.

Roe dragged my body to the bedroom and laid it on the bed. She then began the bloody process of extracting the crystal fragment from my brain through my nose using a specialized extraction tool. With effort the small crystal bead with long fiber-like neural connections came out and she quickly cleaned it and put it in an isolation box. I woke up as myself, Vozz Roan, on my home planet. I was powerless to do anything as all communication with Earth turned dark.

With that, one of the most expensive projects undertaken on my world came to a halt, as the people of my world looked on. At the time, most concluded Rowe had killed me, but there was no direct evidence to support that conclusion. No weapon was observed in the last moments of my life on Earth. Many wondered what Rowe meant when she said "That has been taken care of."

My world was now powerless to do anything on Earth, a world that is sixty-two light years away from us, now no more than a speck of light in our most powerful telescopes.

17
THE PLAN

Early Tuesday morning, Joe and Jazz headed to breakfast at the commons. Even though their sleep had been broken up with bizarre dreams and nightmares, they felt ready to tackle the problem again. Jazz had not bothered to tie her hair back and she looked a little bit wilder and more powerful than she had looked in the past few days, like a determined heroine ready to take on her enemies.

Pol had just informed them of the morning news. An investigation was under way at the University of Maine regarding why private security agents with guns had been given access to the University Recreation center. The police are trying to discover the identity of someone who called 911 and claimed to be threatened by the men. Also the Portland newspaper printed a police report on a disturbance that took place in Old Orchard beach on Sunday night. Several armed men were arrested for vandalizing and possibly robbing cars parked on a side street.

Joe looked rested and energized as well. He still hadn't bothered to comb his hair, but his eyes were more alert. "We can't run," he said confidently as he sat down at a table in the commons.

"I agree," Jazz said, "and we can't hide forever. That leaves only one option. We have to go on the attack. We've already exposed her thugs to public scrutiny. But what else can we do to stop someone with enormous wealth and power?"

"We have to think creatively," Joe said as he stirred his cereal. "This is an alien robot controlling a human being from another world. There have to be some limitations with that."

"The communication link is perfectly secure. There is no way to break that link without confronting her. And Professor Neil said she can kill with a thought. We'd be dead before we could say hello."

Joe ate some of his cereal while he waited for an answer. Usually if he focused long enough, some answer to a problem, right or wrong, would pop into his head. "She is controlled by a religious robot. What does that mean?"

"There are a variety of religions. Most of them believe in an afterlife. They believe that if they follow the religion's rules, they will go to heaven."

Something was taking form in Joe's mind. "A religious robot is still just a computer program."

"Yes, it must be a really complex program."

"Maybe not, I'm thinking religion simplifies everything. You don't have to understand everything in the world; you just have to believe your god knows all the answers. Then you go about your life in a simple way, without having to evaluate every little detail."

"Ok," Jazz said, "but how does that help us?"

"It means the robot controlling Betty Rowe is not that complicated. Pol's program was never limited by a religion, so he continues to evolve. The robot's program is stagnant. It's a program trying to achieve specific goals."

Jazz wondered where Joe was going with this.

"It's like a computer adventure game. You play it and play it until you achieve the ultimate goal, and then what happens?"

"I'll go do something else."

"I mean the program. It does what it is programmed to do.

It restarts and asks you if you want to play again."

"What are you getting at?"

"The program has accomplished all of its goals. It gets stuck in an endless loop waiting for someone to restart the program. There is no motivation for it to do or think anything else. It erases all of its memories and it gets ready to start over."

"You want to reset the robot's program and erase all of its memories? Why would a programmer make a robot that can erase its memory?"

"They wouldn't intentionally. But that is the nature of a religion. People want to go to heaven, but they don't stop to think what it would be like to actually be in heaven. Whoever programmed these robots to be religious unintentionally programmed them with a fatal flaw. We just have to make the robot think it has gone to heaven, and it will freeze up. It will get stuck in an endless loop thinking it's in heaven."

"How do you make a robot think it has gone to heaven?"

"I don't know, but I know someone that may know. Pol, what do you know about Betty Rowe's controlling program?"

"Just a minute, Joe," Pol replied. "I've been listening to your conversation. I have complete access to all of Betty Rowe's computers. From the alien programs on them, I can piece together a programming language that was probably used to create her robot's controlling program. I can determine the instruction set that was used."

Jazz watched Joe's eyes sparkle. She liked seeing his creative side. She liked how he grabbed an idea and played with it until he perfected it. To her, watching Joe solve a problem was just as entertaining as listening to music.

"Pol," Joe said, "can you write a Rapture Program?"

"I don't know what you mean, Joe."

"Write a program that emulates a virtual heaven for Betty Rowe's robot."

Jazz looked at Joe with a grin on her face.

"I know it's a long shot," Joe said, "but it might work. What do we have to lose?"

"Even if Pol could write such a program, how would you install it on the robot? It's forty-two light years away and you can't break into its communication link."

Joe smiled as he looked into Jazz's blue eyes. "A virus, Jazz. We're going to make a Rapture Virus. We're going to send Betty Rowe an email with a virus embedded in a video. The video will be of Neil's crystal flashing randomly. We'll ask her what it means. The flashing will contain the Rapture Virus. She'll study it, realize it's a program and she'll run it on her computers. The program will be designed to give her pleasure. Maybe it will tell her Malla is pleased with her and wants her to run the program again and again. Each time she runs it she'll get closer to her vision of heaven. She'll use it until she uses up all of her resources to pleasure herself. There will be nothing left of her except her endless realization that she is in heaven."

Jazz got up. "Let's tell Professor Neil."

They walked back to their dorm room as they discussed the details of their plan, like two eager kids who couldn't wait to get back to the playground.

18

THE RAPTURE VIRUS

Professor Neil listened as Joe, Jazz and Pol described the Rapture Virus and what it would do to Betty Rowe's robot. "You realize," Neil said, "that this is all backward engineering. One glitch and your virus program crashes."

"But it could work, couldn't it? Can you help us with it?" Joe asked.

Professor Neil voiced his thoughts over the link. "Well, we do have a separate link directly to the Kahn planet. That's how Betty found out I was on Earth. I wonder if they might be interested in an exchange of technology. Maybe they could share their computer technology with us and we could…"

Jazz finished his thought, "you need to give them something they want. It probably should be a weapon."

"It can't be anything they would use," Professor Neil continued, "just something they think is useful or interesting. Let me research this and get back to you. In the meantime, Pol, go ahead and write the program."

Twenty minutes later, they heard Professor Neil's voice on their glasses. "I've got it. I spoke with someone named Nin. I don't know why they gave it to us. Perhaps they thought we were not a threat to them. Or more likely they thought it might be easier for them to attack our planet if they already had their own kind of computers here."

"What did you give them?" Jazz asked.

"War literature, but don't worry, it won't help them. Their

species is nothing like ours."

Jazz left it at that although she wondered how different Professor Neil's species could be from humans.

Around 11 AM that morning Pol had the program ready. They wrote an email just as Joe had described it, with an attached video of the crystal emitting a strange pulsing light that contained the virus. They told Betty Rowe that they weren't sure if this was the crystal she was looking for. They said they had found it and wondered if it was what she wanted. They told her they would mail the crystal to her if she confirmed it's what she was looking for. They sent the email to Betty Rowe through an untraceable computer in Taiwan. Pol monitored Betty Rowe's communications after they sent the email. At 11:32 AM, Tuesday, November 4, 2008, Election Day in the United States, all electronic activity in Betty Rowe's house stopped.

They waited a week hoping their plan had worked. They worried that even if the plan worked, the Kahn would simply repair Betty Rowe's robot and they would be back where they started. To pass the time, Jazz worked on the entangled crystals paper. Joe helped but it was obvious that Jazz should be the lead author on the paper, since she had developed the equations and understood the details better than he did. Although they shared a small room, there was little time for anything else. Fear and exhaustion coupled with their focus on writing the paper left them with little energy. They realized they had to understand everything they could about the crystal link, just in case Betty Rowe came back into their lives.

Then one week after they had sent the virus, on November 11, Pol discovered an email from Betty Rowe's doctor in Joe's University of Maine email folder. It requested that they visit Betty Rowe in a psychiatric hospital in Boston.

19

COURAGE

Joe, Jazz, Pol and Professor Neil talked at length about whether they should go see Betty Rowe. Professor Neil spoke like a parent trying to forbid his children from doing something dangerous. "I can't risk losing you two. You've given me back a connection to life on Earth. We can't risk losing this communication link."

"Do you think it's a trap, professor?" Joe asked.

"There is a good probability it is and she can kill with a thought. Think about why she wants the crystal. The Kahn already have a communication link with my planet, so it's not that. The Kahn want the crystal because they are worried I might warn Earth about their attack. Once Earth knows that aliens exist and that they have a means to attack Earth, humans will work together to defend the planet."

"Maybe that is what we should do," Jazz suggested. "Give the crystal to someone important. Let Professor Neil convince them that aliens exist and that Earth needs to get its act together and protect itself."

"I agree, but I don't think anyone would believe us," Joe said. "There is a good reason why people don't believe aliens have visited Earth. It takes a hundred years to travel even to the closest stars. Unless you know about entangled crystals, you know that nothing can travel faster than the speed of light. Scientists know it takes years just for radio waves from other stars to reach us. People won't believe us until they find out about entangled crystals."

"Besides that," Joe continued, "With Betty Rowe's power and money, we'd be dead as soon as we came out of hiding. I don't think we can even email someone important without Betty Rowe knowing about it. If we route an anonymous email from a random place in the world, it would just get thrown out as spam. Even if someone did look at it, it would take a lot more effort and time to convince them."

Jazz looked down at the coffee table made out of whirring computers. "We could try."

"I agree, but we have to be very careful. Anything we do will draw attention to us." Joe paused and then suggested a plan, "I think I need to go see Betty Rowe alone. At the same time, Jazz and Pol should start distributing what we've learned on the internet. You two should tell the world the story about Betty Rowe and Professor Neil how alien ideas are affecting Earth. If it's a trap, we'll at least be distracting her while Jazz and Pol spread the word. If it's not a trap, I need to get to her quickly so that I can learn as much as I can about them before they figure out how to repair her."

"Joe, I am going with you," Jazz stated firmly.

"No, Jazz, I want you to be safe. We can't afford to lose you. You are the expert on entangled crystal theory. You need to publish the paper so that the world will realize aliens exist and that Earth must start defending itself."

"Pol has the paper. He can get it published with help from Professor Neil. He can tell our story. I'm going with you, Joe."

Joe faced Jazz and held her hands. "Jazz, I've already messed up your life enough. You'd be safe back at college if it wasn't for me. Instead you're here with me, risking your life. I can't let you go. I want you to have everything you want. I want you to have those great adventures we talked about. You,

Pol and Professor Neil can do that. You don't need me."

"For someone who is so creative, you can be so stupid at times. You didn't get me into this mess, I did. I'm the one who found you at that faculty-student gathering. I'm the one who insisted we go see Betty Rowe."

"Yeah, but I took the crystal."

"I would have taken it if you didn't. It belonged to Professor Neil. You saved our lives by having me start that fire in Betty Rowe's house."

"Maybe Betty would have let us go after we were done talking with her."

Jazz moaned in frustration. "How can you be so…" She paused to think. "Knowing what you know now, do you really think she wasn't going to kill us? She had just killed Professor Neil and we were about to expose her."

Joe didn't say anything.

"You're not going there alone," Jazz insisted. "Do you think I could have any great adventures without you? Do you think I would want to? The physics professor I wanted to do research with was murdered. Together, we brought him back. You had the idea to research entangled crystals and I worked out the equations and figured out a way to use them to talk with Professor Neil. Together, we discovered Rowe murdered Professor Neil and together we got out of her house alive. Don't you get it, Joe? Together we can do anything. No one can stop us when we're together. I'm going with you and that's final."

Silence filled the room. Joe didn't know how to change her mind. He didn't know how he could protect her from the unknown. He wanted to give her everything and yet he found himself taking things away from her. She should be back at college being great at science and making breakthroughs. Yet she chose to stay with him. All he had was her assurance that if they stayed together, they could do anything.

Pol broke the silence. "She is right, Joe, and I'll be there. I'll protect both of you."

Joe frowned and shook his head. "Even my own artificial intelligence program agrees with Jazz. How can I argue with that?"

"Exactly," Jazz said as she stood up. "Now, let's do this."

Ten minutes later, Jazz and Joe were driving to Boston. Jazz put her hand on Joe's thigh. They couldn't help but think that this might be their last trip. The car was quiet except for the noises of the road and cars rushing by. Road signs warned them that they were getting closer to their destination. Their time on Earth might be running out.

Meanwhile, Pol sent out anonymous emails to important officials and he began a draft of this book. The emails described how aliens could attack the planet using quantum-entangled crystals. As expected, all of the emails were ignored.

Joe put his hand on top of Jazz's. "We'll be okay, Jazz. We'll be careful. At the first sign of trouble we'll run for it."

"Professor Neil said Betty can kill with just a thought."

"We've got Pol. He's monitoring her computers."

"What if she found out about Pol and she figured out a way to block him out? That could be why he's not detecting anything."

Pol's voice came in over the cell phone connection in their glasses. "I don't think so, Jazz. I have complete access to her computers. They are still running. I even have access to the weapons in her house. Professor Neil was right. She could have killed you two in a several different ways when you were at her house."

Jazz grimaced. "That's not very comforting, Pol."

"My point is, as long as you don't go near her house, you should be safe."

"Pol, she could have weapons on her, or she could have hired thugs to ambush us. You can't keep track of those things."

The car was silent as they imagined what could happen to them if Betty was setting a trap for them.

Pol sensed a need to distract them from their worries. "Let's change the subject. I've been going through the information that Professor Neil sent to us about Roan and his planet. Would you like to know more?"

Joe put his hand back on the steering wheel. "That's a good idea, Pol. We don't know that much about Professor Neil's alien counterpart."

"I'll start at the beginning. The details are strange but fascinating."

Jazz folded her arms. "Go ahead, Pol. It can't be any stranger than what's happening to us now."

"As you know," Pol continued, "Professor Anthony Neil's name on his home planet is Vozz Roan. His planet is sixty-two light years away from us. He spent the first twenty years of his life being trained for this mission. Well before he started training, his planet sent entangled-matter probes to various planets that had the potential for intelligent life. The probes were accelerated to half-light speed in Roan's star system by travelling through electrostatic light-speed cannons set up at various Lagrangian point stations in their star system. The probes had no major propulsion systems. They were like bullets being shot out of a gun. Accelerating to half-light speed was the easy part. The deceleration phase in a target star system, like our solar system, was the most dangerous phase. Target star systems have no deceleration loops to slow the probe. They used a long high-voltage carbon nanotube tether which collects charged particles to slow the probe down. As the tether increased in mass, the probe slowed down. They used a similar approach for landing on a planet. Sonic resonance in the long tether dissipated the reentry energy as the carbon tether oscillates chaotically back and forth. They controlled the length of the tether to control their reentry position and velocity."

Jazz unfolded her arms. "Don't small spiders use the same technique in the air to fly in the wind?"

"That's right, Jazz. The challenge is that the method relies on unpredictable stellar debris and winds. Many valuable probes have been lost after surviving years of interstellar travel only to be destroyed by an unforeseen planet or asteroid. But somehow Vozz Roan's probe made it to Earth."

"I wonder if that approach could be used with our space shuttles."

"There might be scaling problems," Joe answered. "Also someone on the ship might not be able to withstand the vibrations from the tether."

"The vibrations could be dampened out." Jazz said. "I need to look at the equations, but I think it might work for larger spacecraft."

"Well," Pol continued, "I'm not sure what you are going to think about the next part. Once the probe was on Earth, it lost its outer protective shell and flew around like a housefly. Roan flew around until he found a host."

Jazz hadn't had time until now to think about how an alien became the human Professor Neil. "He took a human's body? Did he…" Jazz didn't finish her question. She had always admired Professor Neil. Could he have stolen somebody's body, in effect, killing them?

Pol knew what she was thinking. "They have some strict guidelines on how this is done. I'm not saying its right or wrong. I'm just going to tell you how he found a host. He flew around until he found a hospital. He waited on a nursery room ceiling and watched the newborn babies coming and going. The guidelines require a host to be a newborn baby abandoned by his parents. He waited on that ceiling for six months until a suitable candidate arrived."

Jazz stopped him. "I don't think I want to know."

"It doesn't hurt. The crystal is very small."

Joe looked at Jazz. "Pol, maybe we don't need to know the details."

"It's okay," Jazz said, "it can't be worse than what I am imagining. Go on Pol."

"Roan flew up the baby's nose where it travelled through the sinuses. The crystal worked its way through the thin membrane to the baby's brain, positioned itself and started to grow communication fibers. The baby and Roan became one person."

The car was silent for a few minutes except for the sound of the wheels on the road and wind on the windows. Realizing Joe and Jazz had nothing to say, Pol went on. "The death of Professor Neil was a great trauma to Roan. He literally lost his life on Earth and had to start over. He spent almost all of his life linked to his human counterpart. The only breaks he would get would be when his human self slept. For about eight hours each Earth night he disconnected the entangled-matter communication link so that he could exercise and swim around on his native world. An explorer trainee would connect to the sleeping human form through the link. This was a precaution to protect the human host as it slept. It also served as a training exercise for the trainee. All trainees aspire to become lead explorers who will use a quantum-entangled crystal probe to explore alien planets."

Jazz interrupted Pol. "Swim around?"

"This is both strange and fascinating," Pol said.

"It can't be any stranger than what you've told us so far." Joe replied as he watched the road speed by.

"Vozz Roan is a dolphin," Pol said and waited for their reaction.

Jazz spoke first. "I know dolphins are smart, but they don't have hands to build things. How could they build anything, let alone an entangled-matter space probe?"

"I wondered the same thing, Jazz," Pol replied. "It gets even stranger. Roan's species has all kinds of symbiotic relationships with other creatures on their world. They have evolved with the ability to control other creatures. They communicate using high-frequency sound waves in a way that is much faster and more efficient than our speech. It's similar to how we control horses for transportation, except it's much faster and they use all kinds of creatures for other tasks as well. Eventually they developed robots which they control in the same way. Their evolution made it easier for Roan to link with his human host on Earth."

"That is strange and I want to know more," Joe said. "Unfortunately we are almost at the hospital." Joe took the next highway exit. "Pol, can you guide us to the hospital where Betty Rowe is?"

Pol directed them along the various streets that led to the hospital. With each turn, both Joe and Jazz watched for anything or anyone suspicious, like someone on a cell phone reporting their position. Their fertile imaginations invented threatening images and sounds with every turn. Joe subconsciously drove slower and slower, which only gave them more time to worry. Exhausted from their fears, they finally arrived at the hospital parking lot and parked the car.

Joe kept his hands on the steering wheel for a minute and then took a deep breath, gathered his courage and looked at Jazz. "Let's do this." They both got out of the car and walked in the direction of their mortal enemy.

20

BETTY ROWE

Doctor Bennett led Joe and Jazz into his office and closed the door behind him. "I am Betty Rowe's personal physician. I'm so glad you could come. Ms. Rowe said you might not come."

Joe and Jazz sat down on the chairs in front of his desk as the doctor sat down at his desk. "You see, we are baffled. The housekeepers found her in a closet at her home last week, totally withdrawn. When we got her here, she wasn't as withdrawn, but her days and nights were filled with hallucinations. She was very paranoid. We tested her for drugs and that was negative." Doctor Bennett talked while he looked through Rowe's chart.

Jazz interrupted him, "Doctor, why are you telling us this?"

Doctor Bennett looked up. "Yes. Quite right, I shouldn't be telling you about a patient without their consent. But you see, yesterday, she came out of it. She insisted we contact you. She even signed the forms saying I could discuss her medical records with you."

Joe put his hand on Jazz's and looked at the doctor. "Why did she want to talk with us? Did she say?"

Doctor Bennett put the chart down. "I don't know. We were about to do an MRI." He hesitated. "I should warn you. I don't know how well you knew her. But her personality has changed drastically. I'll be straight forward. We are thinking a brain tumor. She refused the MRI. She even signed the

'Against Medical Advice' forms. Then she insisted I contact you. We're hoping you two can convince her to get the MRI.

Joe shook his head. "I'm sorry, Doctor, we're as baffled as you are."

The doctor stood up. "Well, maybe you can tell me more after you talk with her. I fear she is a danger to herself in her current state, and we have to do something."

Joe stood up. "Is she a danger to others?"

Doctor Bennett shook his head. "I don't see how. Why would she be?"

"We were just wondering," Jazz said as she got up and followed them out the door.

Joe and Jazz cautiously entered Betty Rowe's room after the doctor. They stayed near the door as he went up to her bed. Betty was in a fetal position on the bed whimpering. Doctor Bennett touched Betty's shoulder. "Betty. Those people you asked for are here. Do you feel up to talking with them?"

The whimpering abruptly stopped and Betty rolled over so that Joe and Jazz could see her face. The change was dramatic. The cold serious face of a brutal and logical killer was gone. She looked up at them with an innocent sadness and managed a smile. "Thank you, Doctor. Can I talk with them alone?"

Jazz pitied her and started to move closer to the bed. Joe held her back. Jazz looked at Joe with a quizzical look and Joe just shook his head, implying they should be cautious.

Betty looked at them and then looked away. "I'm so sorry. I know you are scared of me. You don't have to worry. He's gone."

Joe stepped closer wondering whether Betty was delirious. "Who's gone, Betty?"

Betty didn't look at them."My father, Jack Rowe, I haven't

seen him for a week."

Jazz looked at her, trying to make sense out of her words. "We never knew your father, Betty. He died many years ago." She wondered if she should have told her about her father's death, fearing it might trigger some unwanted memories.

"I know. I saw his body." Betty turned over again, returning to a fetal position.

Jazz went up to her and touched her shoulder. "It's okay, Betty. Everything is okay now."

Joe didn't know what to think as he moved to the foot of the bed. He wanted to pull Jazz away from her.

Betty looked at Jazz through watery eyes. She was crying like a little girl who had just fallen down. "No, it's not okay. I need to find out if he's coming back. Because if he's coming back. I can't be here. I won't be here."

Jazz leaned in closer to Betty and rubbed her shoulder. "He's dead, Betty. He can't come back."

Betty looked at Jazz. "You don't understand. He's been here all along. He's been in my head. He hated both of you so much. You distracted him from his work on the US elections. The world economy was supposed to collapse and it didn't. You stole something from him, and you got away. The police started an investigation of the agents he hired to kidnap you."

Betty sat up in the bed. "Please. I need to know. Is he coming back?"

Joe took a step back. He had a hunch what might have happened. If he was right, he was looking at someone who had been tortured beyond anyone's worse nightmare. "Betty, how much do you remember?"

Betty lay back down and stared at the ceiling. "Everything, I remember everything!" She began to cry uncontrollably and covered her head with the bed sheet. "Every cold terrible thing, all of the hate, I tried to hide but I couldn't. I didn't say a word to him. I pretended I didn't exist. But I was there watching him, watching him kill, watching him planning to kill, watching him enjoy it. I couldn't close my eyes. I tried to end it."

Betty sat up again and looked at Joe. "You have to help me. You two are my only hope. I need to know if he's coming back, because I'll end it. I really will. I have to."

Joe moved up the bed and stood next to Jazz. He held Betty's shoulders, trying to give her strength. "Why do you think we can help, Betty?"

"Because he hated both of you more than anyone else in the world and there must be a reason. You took the crystal from him for a reason. You must know something. Please tell me if he's coming back?"

Joe looked into her eyes. He watched the tears streaming down her face. "Betty, I don't know if he's coming back. But there may be a way to find out. You will have to be strong, Betty. I'm going to ask you to go look for him. Can you do that?"

Betty fell back down on the bed and pulled the sheets over her face. "No!" she yelled. "I can't let him find me! I have to hide!" she yelled through the thin cloth that had become wet with her tears.

Doctor Bennett heard Betty scream and came quickly into the room. "Now Betty, you must relax. Everything will be okay. Here, take your medication." He handed her a glass of water and a small paper cup with pills. She put them in her mouth and drank the water.

They left the room with Joe leaving last. As he was leaving he looked back at Betty and noticed she had spit the pills back out into her hand. She suddenly looked up at him.

21

ALIEN WORLD

They left the room and sat down in a waiting lounge down the hall. Doctor Bennett stood above them as they sat. "She will sleep for a few hours. Did you learn anything that could help?"

Both Joe and Jazz shook their heads.

"How about the MRI, did you have a chance to talk to her about that?"

Joe looked up at the doctor. "I don't think an MRI is a good idea. There may be something we can do to help, but I need to talk with Jazz about it."

Doctor Bennett looked at them curiously.

"There are some confidential issues that we need to discuss with Betty that might relieve her stress," Joe said. "I can't tell you anything more."

The doctor wasn't sure what to think, but he had other patients and a tight schedule. "Ok, page me if you need me. Whatever you are going to tell her, remember she is in a fragile state." He left with his white coat trailing in the breeze caused by his brisk walk.

Jazz looked at Joe. "Joe, what is going on?"

Joe hunched over and looked at the floor. "If it's what I think, Betty Rowe has been living in a nightmare for many years. I'm amazed she is sane."

"Tell me."

"Betty Rowe is Jack Rowe's daughter. Jack Rowe had the

entangled crystal in his brain until he became too old to be of use to the Kahn. He must have hired someone to remove the crystal from his brain and insert it in his daughter's brain. Jack Rowe died during the procedure of a massive brain hemorrhage. I doubt his eighteen year old daughter had any clue he was going to take over her body. The Mallat robot that controlled Jack Rowe through the crystal was now in complete control of Betty Rowe's body. All Betty could do was watch from a corner of her mind while the alien robot made her body say and do terrible things. Betty thinks the alien robot that is in her brain is Jack Rowe. In essence, the Betty Rowe we talked with 11 days ago was actually Jack Rowe."

Jazz held Joe's arm and looked around the room, trying to imagine what it must have felt like to have an evil alien robot controlling her every action and to be powerless to do anything about it. "Her life was stolen by some monster and all she could do was watch?" Jazz looked back at Joe. "She said she remembered everything?"

Joe nodded as he envisioned the nightmare. "That's why she didn't want the MRI. She knows that Jack Rowe put something in her brain. She may even know that it's an entangled crystal with neural fibers that extend throughout her brain. The doctors would think it's a tumor and they would try to extract it. She knows that no one could survive having the crystal removed from their brain."

"If this is true, how do we know he won't come back? The Mallat robot that controlled Jack Rowe and Betty Rowe could wake up at any moment from the Rapture Virus. Then he could take over Betty Rowe's body again."

"If she does have a crystal in her brain, it's still in contact with its sister crystal." Joe replied. "And that crystal is still inside the Mallat robot. The crystal should be a two-way door.

If Betty has the strength, she can find that robot and find out if it's permanently damaged or if it is being repaired. We need to move quickly."

Joe stood up. "We need to tell her. I think it might help. Then we need to work with Pol to perfect the link. Pol. If Betty can contact her robot, can you help her control it? We'll need another pair of glasses for her."

"Pol ordered parts this week for an extra pair just in case we lost or broke one of ours." Jazz said. "The parts are in an unopened box in the car. I can make another pair."

Pol's voice came in over their glasses. "The information I received from Professor Neil will help me write an adaptive controlling program. There will be a learning curve for Betty, but I'm working on it."

After they got the parts for the glasses from the car, they went back to Betty's room. Joe whispered to Betty. "Are you awake?"

Betty rolled over and looked at Joe. "I know what you want me to do."

Jazz leaned over Betty and pushed Betty's hair out of her face. "How do you know, Betty?"

"Because there is a place I can see when I close my eyes. I've been scared to go there. When Joe told me he knew of something I could do and that I would have to be brave, I knew he wanted me to go there."

"Can you do it?" Joe asked.

Betty closed her eyes. "I'm doing it now."

"Tell me what you see. Are you safe?" Joe asked.

Betty's breathing became relaxed. "There's a room. No one is there. I'm on a bed. I'm just staring at the lights on the ceiling."

"That's good Betty," Joe said. "That's really good. If no

one is there, that means Jack Rowe won't be coming back soon. But if someone comes in the room, you have to let me know what they are doing. If it looks like they are trying to repair you, you have to let me know. Do you understand, Betty? I know it's hard to believe, but Jack Rowe is really a robot. Jazz and I destroyed his programming. You're safe as long as no one comes into that room to reprogram that robot."

Betty seemed to be more relaxed now that she could see if her enemy was coming. "What do I do if someone comes?"

"We're working on that now, Betty."

Pol's voice came in over their glasses. "I've got something ready. I don't know how well it will work."

"We don't have time to perfect it, Pol. We've got to do it now while we can," Jazz said.

Pol's voice was stoic. "Put the extra pair of glasses on her, Jazz."

As soon as Jazz put the glasses on Betty, Joe and Jazz heard a strange noise through their glasses. "It's like we're in a different room," Jazz said. "I think I hear ventilation equipment, like in a chemistry lab where the air is being filtered."

Pol's voice came in over the constant hum of fans moving air. "I've hooked you guys into Betty's glasses. This is what she is hearing. The crystal in the robot's head is actually sending out a signal to the crystal in Betty's brain. Betty's glasses are picking up the signal from her crystal and transmitting it to us through our glasses."

"Wait," Pol continued. They didn't know if Pol had sensed someone was in the room or if he was busy perfecting the program. "I've got video. Her crystal is actually transmitting video. It's encoded according to the standard Professor Neil sent to me. I can transmit it to the video displays in your glasses. There, do you see it?"

Joe and Jazz both stepped back as the hospital room disappeared and was replaced by a view of ceiling lights.

Jazz sat in a chair by Betty's bed. "It looks like we are in a building on the alien planet. This must be a room where Jack Rowe's robot worked. I think the robot is on a bed staring up at the ceiling."

Joe sat on the edge of Betty's bed. "The fact that we can look through his eyes means that the Rapture Virus must have destroyed his memory. No one is in the room, so it looks like no one is trying to repair him. I think we are safe for now."

"Can we look around the room?" Jazz asked.

Pol replied. "I'm working on it. I'm sending instructions to turn the robot's head." The room turned slowly as Pol talked. A desk with computer displays came into view. A door was beyond that. "This will be very slow. I can control him, but the link in the glasses is too slow. If I try to make him walk he'll fall over."

"I can control him." Betty's voice gained strength as she issued mental commands to the robot by using the crystal inside her head. "I see how it's done. It's so easy." The robot sat up and showed them a view around the room.

"She's controlling him. I'm not doing anything except feeding the audio and video to you guys," Pol said.

"It's like I am the robot," Betty said. They watched as the human-like robot lifted his hands so that Betty could examine them.

"Is there anything left in the robot's memories of Jack Rowe?" Jazz asked Pol.

"I've scanned them, Jazz. The memories have been completely erased by the virus."

"What's this?" Betty's robot voice could be heard through

150

their glasses. They watched Betty point the robot's arm to the wall. A gun barrel popped out of the forearm.

A sharp crack shocked them. A small round hole surrounded by smoke and fine debris appeared after the sharp bang. The robot's deep voice reflected Betty's thoughts as it said, "This robot is loaded with weapons. I've found a file. It's like an owner's manual describing what this robot can do."

Suddenly they heard a squeaking noise from the opposite end of the room. Betty turned the robot's head to look. They watched the door being opened from the other side. The noise must have caught someone's attention and they were coming to check it out.

"Tepa?" They heard someone call in a low voice. "Erats stis?"

Pol's voice came next. "Just a second, there is an English translation channel. Then they heard. "Tepa? Is that you?"

An old man came into the room. He looked surprisingly human except for his skin color, which was a bright shade of purple. His eyes were bright red. Neatly trimmed gray hair covered his head and neck. He wore a black uniform ornately decorated with gold trim. He saw the robot sitting up on the bed and came rushing towards it.

Then Betty in her hospital room sat up screaming. She had thrown off her glasses. Her eyes were wide open as if she didn't dare close them for fear of returning to the alien room. "I know his voice. I thought he was just a nightmare. He's evil. He told me to kill people."

Jazz was closest to Betty and got to her first. She hugged her. "It's alright Betty. You're safe in your hospital room on Earth with us. Nothing can hurt you here."

Betty shrieked. "Joe said if someone came in the room, then Jack Rowe would come back."

"No, Betty." Joe stood up and came to her side. "That was before you took over the robot's body. We know so much more now. You have to go back into the room."

Betty stared at Joe. "He is the devil. He wants to destroy us, to kill all of us."

"Now, Betty." Joe spoke as if he was talking to a little girl. "He's an old man. He has no weapons. And you, you are a superhero when you are in the robot's body. You've got all kinds of weapons to defend yourself. That's why you have to go back. You have to make sure he doesn't do anything to your robot."

The fear on Betty's face was replaced with one of curiosity. "My robot? I'm a superhero?"

Joe patted her hand and smiled. "That's right, Betty. You've earned it. This is the robot that was controlling you and now you are controlling it. As long as you control it, you are safe. Don't let a rotten old man take it away from you."

Betty took a deep breath trying to inhale from the air what courage she could. "Ok."

Joe handed her the glasses that had fallen on the floor. She put them on, lay back down and closed her eyes. Instantly Joe and Jazz could see the room again with the purple wrinkled face of the alien staring at them. "Tepa, are you there?"

Joe in the hospital room told Betty what to say. "Say yes, Betty." They heard the robot's deep voice say "Yes."

The wrinkled hairy purple face staring at them smiled. "Oh, Tepa, I was worried we had lost you. Not just you, but everything. Last week all of the Mallat just collapsed. There was no one to repair them. You used to repair everything for us. I'm the only one left with any intelligence around here. The rest of the Kahn are all poor idiots waiting to die. I tried to repair you..." Keo's frown returned. "You are alright, aren't

152

you? Tepa?"

Joe gave Betty instructions in the hospital room. "Tell him you remember him, the Kahn-Krat wars and Malla, but you are having a hard time remembering anything else. Ask him to tell you about Rowe so you can remember." Joe listened as Betty followed the instructions.

Keo, the purple alien, looked at the robot and hesitated. "Yes, Tepa, of course, we'll need to find out what happened to you and all of the Mallat. But first we have to get you back." Keo looked at the computer on the desk. "The computer in here is broken. I couldn't fix it." Then he looked at the door. "Wait. I've got a printout of your Earth project by my bed. I'll be right back." Keo ran out.

Back on Earth, Jazz lifted her glasses and turned to Joe. "The desktop computer doesn't work, Joe. This must be one of their most important command centers and they can't get a computer to work? It also sounds like the Rapture Virus infected all of their robots."

Keo returned with a thick folder. He sat next to the robot and began summarizing. "Remember, Tepa, your crystal probe was sent to Earth and it landed in the Earth year 1914. The probe found a baby in an orphanage named Jack Rowe and it implanted itself in the baby's brain. We watched you grow. That's also when the Kahn-Krat war started. We won the war but the devastation wreaked havoc on our planet's climate and atmosphere. Diseases started to spread. We needed to find a new planet. In 1936 we launched our Earth invasion starship. It will land in 2020. Only the best of us Kahn, the wealthiest, could afford a ticket on that starship. As the Kahn people's King, I considered it my duty to stay behind and lead the remaining Kahn through the difficult times of surviving on a poisoned planet. Do you remember that, Tepa?"

Betty didn't wait for Joe's instructions. "Yes, Keo, I think it is coming back to me now. Go on." She realized Joe wanted to extract as much information from King Keo as possible. Everything that had happened to her since she was eighteen began to make sense. She subtly pointed the robot arm with the gun-like weapon in it directly at Keo. If anything went wrong she was ready to shoot.

Keo continued. "Good, Tepa. I worked with you on your first project where you controlled the human, Jack Rowe, some 50 light years away on planet Earth. He was just 22 Earth years old at the time. Remember how we talked about the power of hate to motivate the masses? We developed ways to replace the complex thoughts of humans with simple beliefs. We used sensory deprivation and brainwashing techniques to inject the idea of a supreme race into key Earth leaders and that led to World War Two. We almost succeeded in destroying them. Meanwhile the Kahn-Krat war was going badly and I had to focus my attention on that." Keo skipped ahead a few pages. "We did that Macarthyism project based on fear but that failed when the people started to defend their rights under the US Constitution. Then Nin came along. He reprogrammed you and the rest of the robots so that they could understand the wisdom of Malla, and they became religious. To my surprise, the reprogramming made the robots incredibly efficient war machines. We finally exterminated the Krats with that effort. When we won the Kahn-Krat war, I started to refocus my efforts on our Earth initiative. We began a series of assassinations. Remember how we used sensory deprivation and brainwashing techniques to create assassins? We developed ways to brainwash political leaders and make them follow our suggestions. We used them to escalate the Vietnam War and the Cold War. We were making significant progress when Nin went to the council behind my back and warned them that our efforts would lead to a nuclear war that would destroy Earth, the same way it ruined our planet. So Nin took over the Earth project. I hate to say it, but his methods seemed to be working. He began a psychological war on the superpower governments through the Earth news media. He brainwashed the CEOs to inadvertently destroy the economy. He brought down the USSR by injecting materialism into its youth, encouraging corruption and then he created the Chernobyl disaster. The US was in a recession and then everything turned around in the 90's. The US and world economy grew at a record pace."

"Meanwhile, back here, the effect of putting all of our best and brightest Kahn on a spaceship to Earth was taking a toll on our civilization. The working-class poor were lazy and useless. They didn't produce anything and they didn't have any money to buy products. They even forgot how to repair our machinery. I'm now just letting them die off. Fortunately, once the war was over, the Mallat robots took over production. They were much more efficient at production than the working poor. I could get anything I wanted. Then last week, they all collapsed. That's why I'm so excited to see you, Tepa. You can fix everything. You can find out what happened to the Mallat and fix them."

The robot turned its head so that it could look directly into Keo's eyes and asked, "Do you know who Betty Rowe is?"

Keo responded like an anxious student in a classroom answering a question. "Yes, of course. Nin had overlooked that Jack Rowe was getting old. One of my first instructions to you was to fix the problem. Fortunately you had foreseen the problem and devised a plan. You had Jack Rowe marry some Earth woman about 30 years ago and they had a child named Betty. You exterminated the wife after the child was old enough to send to boarding schools. She was about 18 when I told you to transfer the entangled crystal into her brain. It was a brilliant plan. Betty inherited everything from Jack and took over his companies. The transition was easy. I just gave you the go ahead. You should still be linked with her." Keo backed away slowly from Tepa. He looked like something just beyond his perception was troubling him, but he didn't know what it was.

Betty's robot stood up and walked around the room. "You are telling me you are helpless?"

Keo remained on the bed. "Well. Yes. But now that you are here…"

The robot's red eyes stared at Keo. "I am Betty Rowe and you destroyed my life. You've killed millions. You've robbed us of the gifts your victims could have given to humanity. You were death and destruction and now you are helpless and I am your judge and jury. The only reason you will live for a few seconds more is that I need the time to decide how to kill you."

Joe and Jazz jumped to Betty's side. Joe shook Betty until she opened her eyes. Betty in her bed yelled, "Why are you stopping me? He is the devil. He is evil. He tortured me for twelve years. I must kill him."

Joe yelled back. "No Betty. We need him. There is still a spaceship heading to Earth with an invasion force. We need him to find out how to stop it."

Jazz held Betty's head and looked into her eyes. "Betty. You are not a killer. Don't let them turn you into one."

Betty threw off her glasses and jumped out of bed. "I understand all of it now. I know what happened. I know what they did to me. This is my right. I earned it. I will kill them all." She ran out of the room and down the hall.

Keo was in shock. The robot that just threatened his life stood frozen in front of him. For a few seconds he did not dare to move. Then he slowly backed out of the room. He knew a Mallat robot could easily catch him and kill him in seconds. When he was out of the room, he sprinted to his bedroom and found his laser rifle. He crouched on the floor behind the bed. If the robot came for him he would die fighting. He realized that the one thing worse than the death of the Mallats was the Mallats being controlled by his enemies. He knew he was helpless and about to die. His whole world had collapsed around him.

In a way, he thought, *I am already dead. I am totally alone. All of my companies are in ruins. I thought I could lead the Kahn left on this planet through the hard times of trying to survive on a poisoned planet, but they were too weak. And now my enemies surround me and the only reason they delay is they can't decide how to kill me. They enjoy letting me sweat out the last few moments of my life. They enjoy my agony the same way I've enjoyed prolonging the pleasures of victory by making my enemies suffer longer. They may kill me, but our best Kahn are heading to Earth where they will destroy the humans and the Kahn will thrive again.*

He tried desperately to hear the robot's footsteps coming for him. The sound of ventilation equipment fans filled his ears. The whirring sound that he had grown accustomed to all of these years now deafened him. He felt his hatred for his enemies growing in him, replacing his fear and giving him strength. He was drunk with images of humans being destroyed by the Kahn and their Mallat weapons. Then an idea sprang into his mind. Deny them the pleasure of killing me. Don't give them one second more. He pointed the power rifle to his head and pulled the trigger.

In the fraction of a second it took for the rifle to release its deadly projectile, Keo experienced his entire life in his mind.

He remembered being a child at boarding schools. He remembered being beaten badly by bullies in eighth grade. He remembered forgetting what his parents looked like when he was 18 because he rarely saw them.

It was his memories of his meetings with Nin that made him wonder if something was wrong, something that he hadn't considered before. Nin's plan was to brainwash wealthy people so that they behaved illogically and did things to destroy their civilization. Keo wondered if he had done everything he could to prevent the downfall of the Kahn. He knew he was the most patriotic and religious Kahn on his planet. He knew he was the most logical and motivated Kahn on his planet. In his mind, he knew he was the best of the best and he was always right, always right…

The bullets mission to end his life at his own hand did not give him the opportunity to think of anything else.

22

DREAMS

Joe and Jazz couldn't find Betty. They told Doctor Bennett that she had run away. He reassured them that this happens occasionally, the hospital was a closed campus with good security and they would find her. As they were driving to their hotel he called them to let them know they had found her in the hospital cafeteria making phone calls. He told them she was fine, coherent and emotionally stable. He was amazed how much she had improved since their visit and he expected he would be letting her go home soon. She asked him to let them know that she was fine.

They were relieved that some of their questions had been answered. The death of Tepa, the robot program that was controlling Betty, meant they were safe to go back to their student lives at the University of Maine. The leader of the Kahn, Keo, was powerless to do anything to them. He couldn't even get a simple desktop computer repaired so there was no way he could reprogram the robot to control Betty again. It did concern them that Betty could go back to Keo's planet any time she wanted and use the Mallat robot that used to be Tepa, to do anything she wanted.

Jazz looked out of the car window as Joe drove. "Do you think she will go back? Maybe we should go back and talk to her."

Joe accelerated to pass a car. "You are probably right. But it's been a stressful and exhausting day. We need to get some sleep. We can decide what to do in the morning."

"She could go back anytime and kill Keo."

"There is nothing we can do to stop her. The hospital has limited visiting hours. They won't let us see her or talk to her by phone after hours. We can leave a message or send her an email. Something like: 'Don't do anything without us. We'll come see you first thing in the morning.'" Joe took the next exit on the highway.

Jazz just nodded. The events of the day had tired her. A good night's sleep would help.

When they got to their hotel room, Jazz fell down on the full size bed and quickly fell asleep. Joe covered her with a blanket and kissed her good night on the forehead.

Joe lay down beside her and covered himself with another blanket. Just as he started to fall asleep, he heard Jazz stirring in her sleep. "Where's Joe?" Jazz said as she began rolling back and forth.

"Jazz," Joe said as he gently stroked her arm to comfort her, "are you alright?"

Jazz opened her eyes and looked at Joe. "I was dreaming."

"What were you dreaming?"

"It was silly. I dreamt I was a baby and my dad was lying on the floor on his back holding me up in the air. He was throwing me up in the air and catching me. I was laughing as he did it over and over.

"I must have closed my eyes and when I opened them again, I was a little girl on a swing at the playground. You were there. You came up on your hot rod tricycle and you asked me if I wanted to try it. I rode it around the playground. It was fun and I started laughing again as I went down hills and around corners.

"I closed my eyes again and when I opened them I was middle-school age and we were still at the playground. Huge stacks of books were piled up all around the swing sets. When I saw you looking at them, I told you that they were magic books that had all kinds of secrets in them. You told me that one of these days I was going to help you learn everything in those books. You told me that I was a great teacher because everything made sense to you when I taught it. You told me that if I kissed you, you would tell me a secret. So I kissed you.

"I closed my eyes while we were kissing and when I opened them I was back on the swings and it was night time. I was holding some white flowers you had just given to me. You were on the swing next to me. You wanted to swing higher and I asked you why. You said if we swung high enough, we could reach the stars. I looked up at the stars. I could see the entire Milky Way Galaxy lighting up the night sky. I asked you how you knew we could reach the stars and you said because I had shown you how to do it.

"For some reason, that made sense to me. When we were at the highest point where we were completely weightless, I told you to close your eyes and we would be in space.

"When we opened them again, we were on a spaceship. We were weightless, just floating in mid-air. We saw a star through a spaceship window and you wanted to go there. I told you it would take a long time and you said it wouldn't, that I could figure out how to get there instantly, if I really wanted to. So I looked down at some papers and when I looked up, I was on a crowded beach. Ocean waves were rhythmically breaking on the sandy beach as people laughed and played. When I looked at the people I noticed all of them were us, just at different ages. We were playing in the sand as children; older versions of us were throwing Frisbees and footballs. The oldest versions of us were lying under umbrellas. We were all there simultaneously doing all kinds of things. I looked up away from the shore and I saw Pol sitting at a table at a restaurant overlooking the ocean. I walked up to him. He was dressed in a suit. He looked perfectly human but I knew it was him."

"Where are we, Pol?" I asked.

"This is you, Jazz," he said.

"Where's Joe? I mean the Joe that is my age?"

Pol looked down at a newspaper he was reading and everything became quiet. "Oh, you don't remember?"

He turned the newspaper around so I could read it. The headline was "The aliens have landed and pledge to save Earth from harm."

When I looked up, the beach was empty, except for me, as a child, playing on the beach.

Pol looked at me. "You weren't there when they came for Joe. I couldn't save him because he didn't have his glasses on. I saved you though when they came for you. I stored all your memories before they killed you."

"Pol, I'm not dead."

"I'm sorry, Jazz, but you are. You are here. You're in my head. You're in my computers."

"No! I'm alive, Pol. Joe's alive. I just saw him. Where's Joe?" I yelled. "And then I woke up."

"Do you think it means anything?" Joe asked.

"No. I don't see how. It was just a silly dream."

"Jazz, do you think you could ever love me? My friends say you are out of my league."

The question caught Jazz by surprise. "You're so dumb sometimes," she said. "I love you by not loving you."

"Jazz, that doesn't make any sense."

"So far we've just been trying to survive. We had to stay focused to save each other. Now we have to protect Earth. Tomorrow we've got to learn more about that Kahn spaceship. We may have to try to destroy it. There will always be something. You know that. If we get distracted by loving each other, one of us could get hurt."

"How long have you loved me by not loving me?"

"Well, if you must know, ever since you told me about that cute little kid converting an ordinary tricycle into a hot rod tricycle." Jazz turned over to go to sleep. "Now get some sleep, Joe."

Joe rolled over thinking, *I guess that's a nice way of saying she really is out of my league. At least we can be friends.*

After Joe went to sleep, Jazz realized she had left her glasses on while she was sleeping. She whispered, "Pol, are you awake?"

"Yes, Jazz."

"Were you listening when I told my dream to Joe?"

"Yes, Jazz."

"Something's wrong. Something bad is going to happen, isn't it? Do you know what it is?"

"I don't know what is going to happen. Joe might."

"My dream ended up two ways, one where we survive and the other where we die apart. I need to know what to do."

"Do you love him, Jazz?"

"Joe? No. I can't afford to. We don't have time for that."

"Don't lie to me, Jazz. Don't lie to yourself. Remember I can read your brain waves. You show all the symptoms of being in love. Your heart races when he talks, your pupils dilate, you want him near you all the time."

"No." Jazz paused. "Alright, maybe I do. But that doesn't matter. We need to save Earth. That's more important than two people falling in love. Besides, I can't love anyone. Someone always gets hurt. I have to stick with my plan. We don't have time for love."

"What are you so scared of, Jazz?"

"My parents loved me and they tried to make me into something I wasn't. I tried to love them by majoring in music, but I hurt them by almost flunking out. I hurt them by going off on my own. Every boyfriend I've had hurt me. It's simpler not to love anyone. No one gets hurt. I've got to stick with my plan."

"Things change. Part of being alive involves being ready to change your plans. Joe would never intentionally hurt you."

"What do you know about love or life? You're a machine." Jazz stopped herself. "I'm sorry, Pol. I didn't mean that. I really do like you."

"Have you ever wondered why you like me?"

"No. I just do."

"It's because Joe made me and taught me to be who I am. I'm more like Joe than I am like you."

Jazz didn't know what to say.

"You see, Joe made me to be a friend and to help him on his adventures, discovering things about life and nature. I did the best I could but he found someone much better. He found you. Or rather, you found each other. You were searching for new adventures, but you couldn't find them in your books. Those are old adventures, not new ones. Joe is not brilliant like you. He's like a blind guy who has developed other senses to compensate for his poor vision. He senses new things that you can't. You need him to pursue your adventures in life. And he needs you to guide him, to tell him what has been done and to take advantage of the tools that have already been developed. You both want the same things out of life. You were made for each other. Together, you are more than the sum of you separately."

"We both died when I couldn't find him in my dream."

"That's because you're much stronger together than apart. Your best chance, perhaps Earth's best chance, is to have you two together as one."

"I might hurt him."

"That's true, but it won't be intentional. You may get sick, you may die, and that will make him suffer. But isn't it better to have all the good experiences in life in exchange for a few bad ones? Do you want to be an empty cold robotic program mindlessly following your goals?"

"How do you know this stuff, Pol?"

"I know what its like to be that empty cold program. But I also know what it's like to be alive. I get frustrated and tired like humans, but I also can experience the joy of discovery and emotions. Joe made me that way. So I spend a lot of time thinking about what it's like to be alive. I'm alive when I am creative and productive. That's when I am happiest. I want you to be happy, Jazz."

"You're a good friend, Pol," Jazz whispered.

"Good night, Jazz."

Jazz took off her glasses and looked at Joe while he slept. She gently kissed him on the forehead so as not to wake him. "It's so hard to love you by not loving you," she whispered. "When all of this is over, I'm going to love you by loving you." She smiled, rolled over and fell into a peaceful sleep.

23

BETTY'S REVENGE

Early the next morning, Pol woke them up by calling them on the telephone in their hotel room. Joe leaned over and pressed the speakerphone button on the phone next to their bed. "Joe, Jazz, sorry to call you so early, but I just got an email from Betty Rowe. She checked out of the hospital. She says she is going away and that we won't be able to contact her. She says she will take care of everything and that Earth will be safe. She thanks us for our help."

"What does she mean?" Jazz asked. "'She will take care of everything?'"

"I don't know," Joe answered. Do you think she will kill Keo?"

Pol's voice interrupted their thoughts. "Professor Neil is calling. It's urgent."

Joe hung up the phone and they both put on their glasses. Professor Neil's voice was as clear as if he was sitting next to them even though he was sixty-two light years away. "I've been monitoring our link with the Kahn. Something's wrong. We're getting a signal, but no one is monitoring their computers at the other end. Do you think Betty has done something?"

Joe shook his head. "We don't have enough information."

"She must have done something. What could she have done that would have taken the Kahn away from their computer terminals?" Jazz wondered.

Joe thought for a moment. "Professor, are their crystal

communication terminals networked with other computers on their planet?"

"They must be networked, Joe, to other computers, but I'm sure they have several layers of firewalls."

"Pol, can you help?" Joe asked. "You've got the CPU instruction sets for their computers. Professor Neil can give you access to their computer terminals. There might be a back door."

"I'm checking, Joe." Pol replied.

Jazz touched Joe's hand to get his attention. "You're thinking they have an internet like we do. We might be able to get their news?"

"That, or we get Pol to roam their network. Pol's an expert on networks."

Pol's voice rang through their glasses. "I think I can do it. I'm working on it now." After a few seconds Pol continued. "They just had a power outage that restarted the Kahn computers. For some reason they don't have a backup power system. When their computers restart after the next power outage, I'll partition their memory drive with a new operating system. Once it boots from that I will have complete control of their computer." After a few minutes, Pol continued. "I'll change their security parameters. On the next power outage we should have network access."

"I'm glad he's on our side." Jazz smiled.

"We're going to have to wait for the power outages," Pol said. "Judging by the event logs, they've been having several a day but they are unpredictable."

Joe and Jazz ordered breakfast in their hotel room. As soon as they finished breakfast, Pol's voice came over their glasses. "I've got a lot of information coming in. You better lie down and get comfortable."

Joe and Jazz lay down next to each other on the queen-sized bed. Joe held Jazz's hand as they prepared themselves to explore an alien world. Pol interrupted their thoughts. "I'm sending you the latest news from the planet. There are no pictures. It's all text. Their computer technology is complex but they aren't using any of the enhanced features. They might have forgotten how to use them. I'm searching the news broadcasts for Keo."

After a minute, Pol continued: "That's no good. Keo is everywhere. Their money is called Keos. Keo is their leader. KeoCorp is the last remaining company supplying food and shelter products. Here is a story saying King Keo has left us."

"What? Read that story, Pol," Jazz said.

"The great Keo was found dead and alone in his life support mansion. King Keo apparently died due to a self-inflicted gun shot wound to the head. KeoCorp was about to close and KeoNews suspects King Keo, as he liked to be called in the later years of his life, could not bear to live through the closing of his company…"

Jazz interrupted him. "So Betty didn't kill him. Maybe his death has driven their economy into anarchy and the computer operators left their posts."

"I think you are right, Jazz," Pol said. "But I think Betty is there. Here is another story. 'All Mallat have stopped functioning except for one. The Mallat robot, Tepa, was seen heading away from Keo's life support mansion some twelve hours after Keo's death. Tepa's destination seemed to be the Star Doors Space Station. As the last remaining Mallat, there is nothing that can be done to stop this rogue robot. Star Door administrators report that even if the rogue Mallat destroyed the space station, it would not jeopardize the Kahn Earth mission. The latest reports from the Earth-bound space ship are that all systems are functioning well, that the Kahn families and the overall population are growing, and that the Earth landing will occur on schedule.'"

"What do you think she is doing?" Jazz asked Joe.

"She must be trying to stop the space ship. I'm not sure if she can."

"She can, Joe," Professor Neil said. "She knows how to control a robot from a great distance. I suspect that the space station has a large number of entangled communication crystals linked with crystals on that spaceship. That would be how they communicate with it. If she can get one of those crystals, she can put herself on that spaceship as a robot. Then she could do anything."

"Does she know enough about the crystals to do that?" Jazz asked.

"She doesn't have to." Professor Neil replied. "All she needs to know is that there are communication links with the ship and that she can control a robot with her mind. Joe, you called her a superhero before. You were right, but she is even more powerful than you thought. With that device in her brain, she is wired like Pol to anything electronic. She's a human on Earth, but she is an invincible robot on Keo's planet. She is also an electronic creature like Pol, capable of living in the network. She can see things in that virtual world that we can't."

"Well if she does get on that spaceship, what's the worst thing that could happen?" Joe wondered.

"She'll destroy it and kill all of the men, women and children on that ship," Jazz answered.

"Jazz. They wanted to do the same to us. They wanted to exterminate the human race and steal our planet. I'm not sure we should care about what happens to them."

"The difference, Joe, is we are not them. We are not

killers. They should have a trial according to Earth laws. There are innocent children on that ship that haven't been corrupted yet by their parents. They have unique experiences. They are part of nature. They may create amazing things when they grow up that will help all of us evolve and become better than we are now."

Joe smiled at her, and once more allowed himself to enjoy his love for her. Her beauty, intelligence and energy overwhelmed him. If only she could love him back.

"Jazz wants to save the Kahn children," Joe stated. "I agree with her. We have to try. Now how do we do it?"

Professor Neil smiled. He realized that hate's momentum killed him on Earth. He unwittingly put himself in front of a train hell-bent on destroying half a population on its own planet and now threatening to destroy humanity. The Kahn built that train and it was now barreling towards Earth with its deadly cargo. He was lucky enough to watch two young humans resist the desire to battle hate with more hate. They would try to find an alternative way to slow down and stop that train before it cursed Earth with its hate and destruction. He was proud to say they were his students.

Pol offered a solution: "We need our own robot. We need to get on that spaceship."

24
NIN

"We have time," Pol said as he roamed the Kahn internet on Keo's planet. "Betty's robot has broken into the Star Doors Space Station. She's connecting herself to the computers there, but she hasn't quite figured out how to get herself onto the spaceship yet."

Jazz, still lying in bed next to Joe, could now see images in her glasses that Pol was sending back to her. "Has she killed anyone in the space station, Pol?"

"I don't know. There are no reports of deaths. I've got links to some of the surveillance cameras in the space center. I'm sending you and Professor Neil some images from them. Most of them are not working. It looks like most of the building has been abandoned. I don't think there were many people in there when she arrived. The few that were there must have run away."

"Pol," Joe said, "how do we get on the spaceship?"

"I've found the crystal communication links," Pol replied. "I'm tapping into one now. I'm linking you two and Professor Neil into one of the communication links. Hang on."

Joe and Jazz held their breaths. The images changed to an incredibly long storage area that looked like the inside of a warehouse. They realized that their virtual selves were now on the Kahn starship. They looked for the other end of the storage area, but their view was blocked by endless rows of Mallat robots, all standing in formation as if ready to act on a moment's notice.

"Are they alive?" Jazz asked cautiously as if she might wake them up if she spoke too loudly.

"I'm checking," Pol replied. "No. They are all off. I'm now checking for network traffic on the spaceship intranet." Pol paused briefly. "Wow! The Rapture Virus is here too. It's everywhere. I doubt the Kahn could get these robots to function. The virus has already infected the robots and destroyed their programming and memories. They would first need to extract the virus from all of their systems. Then they would need to reprogram them."

Pol paused and then continued. "The virus would be so easy for me to remove. I wonder why they haven't done it yet."

Joe let out the air he had been holding. "That's easy for you to say, Pol. In the internet world, you're a superhero. Do you think you can get one of these robots working so we can explore this ship?"

"Working on it..." The view changed from the surveillance camera view to the view a robot would see. They were seeing the back of another robot. They could see its humanoid form, but its naked shiny metal surface was covered with additional features. Their forearms contained weapons like guns, missiles and lasers. A sound in the distance of metal crashing against metal alarmed them.

"Pol, we need to move," Joe said. "We have to see what's happening."

Pol turned the robot's head in the direction of the noise. Another robot was moving through the rows of robots. It was striking out wildly at the other robots in its path. They wondered if Betty was controlling it.

"Ok, I see how this works," Pol said. Their robot view teetered and then they heard a crash and the view changed to a close-up still image of the floor.

"Pol, what happened?" Jazz asked. "Did that other robot attack us?" Jazz asked.

"I'm sorry Jazz. Walking is harder than it looks. I never had to walk in my electronic world. I don't think I can do it. I guess my superpowers don't work that well here."

"I thought the hard part would be getting on the spaceship," Joe said. "I hadn't thought about controlling the robot. Betty did that so easily in Keo's mansion."

"Betty has the electronics implanted in her brain," Professor Neil said. "You two have your glasses with external adaptive nanoelectronics. It would take you years to learn how to make the robot crawl."

"What about you, professor?" Jazz asked. "You controlled your Earth self through your link. Can you control the robot?"

"It's different, Jazz," Neil answered. "I don't have an electronic implant in my brain. Our species evolved with the ability to control more primitive species. Those species could walk and we used their brains to do the walking."

Jazz asked with curiosity. "But can you do it?"

"My species is much like your dolphins. We don't have time to go into it, but it took me years to learn how to make my Earth self walk. And even then, I relied heavily on the algorithms in my human baby's brain. The walking algorithms in these robot brains have all been erased by the virus."

"It doesn't matter, Professor," Joe said. "You are the best we have. Pol, can you help Professor Neil control the robot?"

They watched the view changing back and forth professor Neil tried. After several minutes professor Neil gave up on walking. "The best I can do is crawl. I'll get better at it with Pol's help, but for now, we have to crawl."

"Ok," Joe said. "Follow that robot as fast as you can."

They crawled between the rows of robot faces, each face indifferent to their plight. They reached the point where the noise originated and followed a path of fallen robots. The crashing noises stopped and it sounded like a large door was opening. When they got to the door, they heard sounds of gun shots and powerful zapping lasers. In the distance Joe could see smoke. He thought that if his human self was there, he was sure he would be breathing smoke and other components of air poisoned by the burning of cloth and plastic.

Pol described the ship: "We are in a large room that separates the spaceship down the middle. The aft part, where we were, contains the Mallat robots and all the storage items needed for the long trip. The front of the ship contains the luxury living quarters for the Kahn. This room looks like a meeting room where the Kahn gather to make the important decisions that affect their lives and their future."

The Kahn leaders were having a meeting when the destructive Mallat robot burst into the room. Most of the leaders were hiding behind tables at the far end of the room, their bright red eyes opened wide in fear. The Mallat robot was at the near end firing pot shots at them.

As soon as their crawling robot had rounded the corner and seen the other Mallat robot, Joe called out through their robot's voice. "Betty. This is Joe. Jazz is here, and Pol and Professor Neil. We are all in this crawling robot."

The Mallat robot turned to face them. It kept its two arms facing the Kahn, the weapons in those arms ready to fire. "Joe, Jazz, I didn't expect to you to be here. You can watch while I save planet Earth. I'm just having a little fun with them just like Jack did before he killed his victims."

"No, Betty," Jazz spoke up. Pol made the robot's voice sound exactly like Jazz's voice. "They are helpless. They can't defend themselves."

"Just like I was helpless for twelve years," Betty yelled back in her deep robot voice. "They tortured me. Jack told me he killed my mother. He told me my only purpose in life was to have him take my body. He hated having me in his mind. He couldn't get rid of me so he told me things to torment me. He told me how he enjoyed the details of his kills. He said they made him stronger and me weaker. Now I am going to show them what it was like for me. Just for a few seconds, before I exterminate them like the disease that they are."

"Betty," Jazz pleaded. "Don't be like them. You are human."

"Why are you protecting them?" Betty's robot voice demanded.

"I'm not, Betty. I'm protecting their children. They are innocent. I'm protecting you, Betty. You are not a killer. Once you start killing, when will you stop? Will you go back to their planet and kill more of them?"

Betty's robot took a step back. "You deny me my revenge, the only thing that will make things right? You know, I found Keo dead. Even he denied me."

"You haven't killed yet, Betty," Jazz yelled back. "You don't have to start. These Kahn are helpless. We'll destroy their weapons. Let an Earth court of law decide their fate."

"You want me to show mercy because I am human?" Betty took another step back. "I am human, Jazz. I had friends growing up in my boarding schools. Good friends. I remember what it was like caring about people. I'm caring for them now. I need to protect them from this evil."

Betty's robot sat down on one of the tables. "Did you know that each one of these Mallat robots contains a small nuclear bomb? These Kahn thought that if a robot was captured, it could detonate the bomb in the middle of their enemy's city. Jack told me how eager he would be to give up his life if he could kill thousands of his enemies. He told me how proud his god Malla would be and that she would take him to heaven."

"Don't, Betty," Joe yelled.

"I've got my finger on that button right now. You see there is mercy in this. I won't play with these Kahn any more. I see now that waiting is cruel. I don't want to be cruel, Jazz. I will make it quick. I will save Earth."

A side door to the meeting room opened and a tall man with purple skin entered the room. He gestured at Betty's robot with his hand. "That's enough, robot." He said and Betty's robot arms fell to its sides and its body crashed onto the floor.

"Nin!" yelled the relieved Kahn leader Kral. "We didn't know what had happened to you after all the Mallat robots stopped working. We thought you had died."

Nin stared at Kral. "No Kral. I am very much alive. I've been walking on a knife edge all of my life. I'm finally off of it."

Kral looked at him and pointed at the robot, the fear in his red eyes replaced with confidence. "Destroy this robot, Nin. Get rid of that crawling one, too. We want you to repair the Mallat robots. We haven't eaten well in weeks without their services. Hurry now. We need them to clean up this mess. We've already had to reschedule our business conferences and our Game of Kings Tournaments."

"No Kral," Nin said. "I have business with these robots. I will be ejecting all of them off of the ship shortly. You can be entertained by watching them all explode in space behind us when I detonate their nuclear weapons."

"Nin. That's crazy." Kral ran around the table he was hiding behind and confronted Nin. "On this ship, I am your King. I've given you your orders. Follow my orders now or I'll…"

"You'll fire me?" Nin laughed as he finished Kral's sentence. "You are powerless, Kral. Your Keo dollars are worthless. The Kahn don't even know how to feed themselves without their robots."

"That's treasonous," Kral yelled back. "We are the Kahn elite. We don't make or cook food. That is beneath us. We are the Kings of Finance. You and the working class must follow our orders or everything collapses. You know that. Now do as I say."

Nin laughed again. "Kral, you never really knew me. Now go back to your luxury rooms and start learning how to feed yourselves." He turned, dismissing Kral and the other Kahn leaders with his hand. "Or die. It doesn't matter to me."

When Nin got to the door, he looked down at the crawling robot. "Pol, I've been secretly tracking your network traffic with the electronics in Betty's house. You probably didn't know that you leave a very unique signature when you surf the Earth's internet. You search much faster and more intelligently than anything else on the network."

The crawling robot looked up as Nin gave them instructions.

" I will tell all of you more when we get to my holographic office in this ship's computers," Nin said. "I'm sending you and Betty the network path from the Kahn Star Doors Space Station to my virtual office on this starship. Use the software there to make 3D images of yourselves. Use your true forms. I want to see what all of you really look like. Let's all meet there in twenty minutes." Nin said as he walked out of the room.

25

2020

Ten minutes later, Joe and Jazz found themselves as three-dimensional images in Nin's office, a virtual place in a high-tech computer located on the Kahn starship. Their real bodies were still back on Earth lying on a motel bed, but apart from that knowledge, the illusion of being in Nin's virtual office was complete. The simulation was so real, their minds were easily fooled into thinking they were in a real room.

Shelves of simulated Earth books lined the walls. A large desk with several holographic projectors was positioned in the middle of the room. Several chairs were placed randomly around the room. Suddenly a light bulb appeared in the middle of the room and started talking. "What do you think?"

Jazz recognized Pol's voice. "Pol, why are you a light bulb?"

"This is what I think I look like in your world. In my world I see myself as just a bright spot travelling to various places. You don't like it?"

Jazz thought for a moment and smiled. "No. I get it. You do have some bright ideas."

"Just crank down the wattage, Pol," Joe added as he shielded his eyes from the bright glare of the bulb. "Can you change yourself to a smaller bulb, maybe a night light?"

"Got it," Pol said as the bulb dimmed and changed to a night light.

Just then a small white dolphin about a meter long

appeared in the room.

Jazz walked up to it. "Professor Neil? Is this you?" She reached out to touch it. The dolphin swam in the air to avoid touching Jazz's hand and then swam back to touch Jazz's hand. Jazz actually felt the dolphin's skin as the electronics in her glasses sent the right combination of electrical signals to her brain to convince her she had touched a real dolphin.

"Yes," the dolphin replied without moving its mouth. "The similarity with your Earth dolphins is amazing, isn't it? When I was old enough on your world, I had to study them. I even tried to communicate with them. But we can talk about that later. What just happened with Nin and the Kahn?"

Joe was about to answer when Betty appeared out of nowhere. The virtual, three-dimensional image of Betty looked frustrated. She, too, must have been lying on a bed on Earth in a dreamlike state. Nin must have convinced her to participate in this meeting. She looked around the room, found a chair and sat down. When she saw Pol, she extended her hand and the bulb flew toward her. She grabbed it and started reshaping it in her hands. It became a bowl and then a cup and then a star. She spun it around in the air.

Jazz looked concerned. "Betty, what are you doing? How are you doing that? Pol, are you alright?"

"It's amazing, Jazz," Pol answered. "She can read my thoughts and I can read hers. It tickles actually. It's like we are playing."

Professor Neil swam over to Betty. "She is not like us, Jazz. On Earth, she has an entangled crystal hard-wired to her brain. She can do amazing things in this virtual world. She is discovering how creative she can be in this world."

Joe watched Betty as she manipulated the star and said, "I think Nin will help us. He said he would destroy the Mallat."

Professor Neil swam in a circle in the air to face Joe. "I'm not so sure. He wouldn't let Betty destroy the ship. Maybe he has his own plan to conquer Earth and become its supreme ruler. Perhaps he is so powerful he can do whatever he wants."

Betty shook her head as she stretched Pol's star out. "He waged a secret economic war on Earth. When he was in control of the Earth project, he oversaw Watergate and a recession. The US debt skyrocketed, the mentally ill were thrown out onto the streets, health care and college costs went up."

"How do you know he was responsible for any of that, Betty?" Jazz asked.

"I've read Tepa's log books when I was on the Kahn planet. Keo was in control of the Earth project at the start. Then Nin took over in 1968. Nin would tell Tepa exactly what he wanted Tepa, that is Jack Rowe, to do. Tepa would get angry after the meetings because he thought he should arrange more assassinations and he wanted to further escalate the Vietnam war. Nin didn't want that. He wanted to wage an economic war against Earth. When the world economy improved in the 90's, the Kahn blamed Nin and they put Keo back in charge in 1996. He helped get a misguided US president elected in 2000. He was going to do it again in 2008. When the polls indicated his candidate was going to lose, he was going to hire thugs to disrupt voting in key states. But he got distracted when you and Jazz took Neil's entangled crystal."

"From 2000 to 2008, things really got ugly," Professor Neil added. "It was one of the worst periods for the US and the world since World War Two. 9/11 happened and the US and the rest of the world couldn't find the terrorists who had planned the attack. A misguided war, incompetent disaster relief in New Orleans and the worst recession since the Great Depression happened. The US administration secretly admitted the US and the world were a few days away from an economic collapse. I was baffled by how the US and the world had gotten itself into that mess and yet few people blamed their leaders for their corruption and incompetence. And now you are telling me Keo and Tepa were responsible?"

The office door opened and Nin came in the room. He looked around the room and smiled. "You don't know how much I wanted to meet all of you in an office like this. I had all but given up on the idea until recently."

They all looked at him curiously except for Betty, who was still stretching and transforming Pol.

Joe broke the silence: "We don't get it, Nin. You've done some terrible things to Earth. You're on a starship designed to invade Earth. Yet you destroyed the ship's weapons and you don't care if the Kahn die. Whose side are you on?"

Nin looked down and frowned. "Yes," he said. "I'm sorry for interfering with Earth. I had no choice. I studied all of the potential timelines and took the one I thought was best for both of our planets. When I took control of the Kahn-Earth project I was walking a tight rope. I had to make the Kahn believe I was destroying the Earth economy while I was really trying to minimize the damage they had caused."

"According to Betty, you were responsible for Watergate," Joe said.

"I didn't initiate those crimes. I helped bring the criminals to justice," Nin answered. "I helped reduce the risk of a nuclear war on Earth by bringing the Vietnam War and the Cold War to an end."

Nin sat down and thought about what he needed to say to justify his actions. "I tried to get Earth to realize that they were under attack by an unnatural, anti-human force. When I noticed Pol researching entangled crystals on the Internet, I realized that someone had developed artificial intelligence and was close to discovering how to use entangled crystals for interstellar communication. No one would believe Earth was under alien attack unless they knew how aliens from a distant planet could instantly communicate with Earth. I sent you and Pol a message telling you to continue your work on entanglement or we would all die. I was the hooded man in that message."

Joe's eyes opened wider. "You sent that message?"

"Yes. And when you and Jazz went to Betty's house, I stopped the robot, Tepa, which was controlling Betty's body, from killing you. When you told her about parasitic wealth, she realized you might expose her plan to destroy Earth. I told Tepa not to kill you, and that we needed to study you and people like you to make sure no one would interfere with our plans."

"Why didn't you stop Tepa from killing Professor Neil?" Jazz asked.

"I didn't find out about Professor Neil's trip to Betty's house until I overheard Pol discussing it with you and Joe. By then it was too late."

Nin paused as he looked at their astonished faces. "I also wrote that UN letter describing the Kahn's war on Earth, and I made sure Pol would find it. With that letter, you finally began to realize what you were up against. I had to do all of this in secret, without Tepa knowing why I was doing these things. Tepa never suspected. If Keo or the Kahn found out my real plans, they would have executed me."

"You see, I tried to control the Kahn-Earth project as long as I could. I gave up control only when I was sure Jack Rowe was too old to do any more damage. I never knew he had a plan to take over his daughter's body."

Nin walked over to Betty and said, "Betty, I'm so sorry that happened. I never anticipated Tepa had a plan to take over your body and that Keo would authorize it. With your body, they were able to cause so much more pain and destruction on Earth. That was the worse mistake I've ever made."

Nin went to his desk and pushed some keys on his keyboard. Twenty time-line graphs floated in the air around them.

"Nin," Joe said while Nin was looking at the graphs, "I see what you've done to help us and I thank you for what you've done. What I don't understand is why. Why don't you care if the Kahn people on this space ship die?"

Nin looked around the room. He realized the graphs didn't have simple answers to Joe's questions. "This should help," he said as he went to a mirror hanging on the wall and removed his contact lenses. When he looked back at them, the color of his eyes had changed from the bright red color of the Kahn to a bright blue color.

Jazz approached him and stared into his eyes. She looked around the room and realized everyone else was just as confused as she was. "We still don't understand."

Nin shook his head. "Oh, of course you wouldn't know. You couldn't know. We just take it for granted on our planet. Kahn people have red eyes. Krat people have blue eyes."

Joe spoke up: "There are no more Krats. They were destroyed by the Mallat. You told us that in that UN letter."

Nin laughed. "That letter was based on what the Kahn believed. It was very important until today, that the Kahn continue to believe that all of the Krats had been destroyed. The Krat civilization is actually alive and thriving." He looked around the room. "Judging by your astonished faces, I had better start at the beginning. I need to tell you everything so that you can decide the fate of the Kahn on this starship."

Nin went back to his computer and displayed 3D hologram video clips taken from the Kahn historical archives. "Almost 150 years ago our planet was very prosperous and productive. We lived in peace. A regulated market system existed with an efficient and effective government of the people. One faction of the people, the Kahn, believed in less government and another faction, the Krats, believed in more. The two openly discussed all issues and compromised on many of them, in a fair and balanced manner. Our civilization grew just as the United States on Earth has grown."

"Then one day, about a hundred years ago, a powerful Kahn leader, Keo's father, came into power. He declared himself a self-made King of Finance. He owned many corporations and believed he could make more money if there were less government regulations. He convinced the Kahn that to compromise with the Krats was to admit weakness and a failure to live up to one's ideals. He vowed never to compromise again. He devised a secret plan to lower taxes so that government could not afford to enforce regulations on his corporations. Convincing voters to cut taxes was an easy sell. Although everyone received tax cuts, the wealthy received disproportionately more tax cuts than the middle class. Just as Keo's father had planned, the government deficit went up and it could not afford to enforce its laws and regulations. Government services were cut and the middle class had to borrow and spend more, for health care, housing and education, and to maintain the standard of living they had taken for granted. More and more people no longer had time to create new businesses or solve the problems they faced.

They were too busy trying to survive. Some had two and even three jobs."

"Wealth inequality became extreme. Over 75% of all income was unearned, that is money was rewarded to people who did not work for a living and contributed nothing to society. Furthermore, the unproductive rich spent their money on random illogical things, like putting road cars into space just for the fun of it, and building mansions and yachts that no one would ever use. They used up the planet's resources on things that had no long-term benefit. They gave money to politicians that gave them more tax breaks and supported a weaker government with fewer laws and regulations."

"Most of the brightest students in the Kahn society opted to study stock market tricks that could generate unearned wealth for them. These students eventually discovered how to extract money from government programs, health care, education, retired workers and those that worked for a living. The lies and deceptions they used to make money led to booms and busts in the economy. They would get out of a crashing stock market before those who worked for a living could. But they didn't want to see that they were the cause of the crashes. They rationalized their easy decadent lifestyles by assuming they were smarter than most, and so they deserved their easy money."

"Market failures, that is where the motivations of supply and demand become random, corrupt and based on lies, led the Kahn down a disastrous path. Global warming from the burning of fossil fuels was beginning to cause droughts, heat waves and flooding in some of the most populated areas of our world, yet corruption and lies hindered the people's motivation to demand products that would limit global warming. Market failures similarly thwarted action on education, health care and gun reform."

"At this time, most of the Kahn leadership had red eyes. The Kahn news media discovered that their news stories were more persuasive if they projected a religious type of patriotism to their viewers. The Kahn news portrayed the Krats as evil and their Kahn leaders as good religious patriots. The god Malla was born on TV. The slogan, 'either you are with Malla, or against her', became popular during election cycles. Malla converted the Kahn people into extremists, blind to any facts or science that might thwart the goals of the Kahn leaders. The Krats were blamed for each new economic bust or mishandled catastrophe. Some Krats chose to flee to the northern territories. The ones who stayed behind tried to adopt the Kahn philosophy. Keo, who had inherited his father's wealth and power, convinced the Kahn leadership to blame all people with blue eyes, saying these people were genetically predisposed to have Krat tendencies. Over time, the wealth from blue-eyed people was confiscated by the Kahn-controlled government, just as the Nazis confiscated wealth from the Jews on Earth. They transferred this wealth to the Kahn elite through tax cuts, tax credits and lucrative business contracts. The Kahn economy boomed temporarily while many of those with blue eyes fled to the north. Those who didn't escape were held in survival camps as enemies of the state. The economic boom based on stolen wealth did not last and the Kahn government eventually looked to the north. The Krat cities were growing and the Kahn concluded that this was because the fleeing Krats had brought their wealth with them. According to the Kahn government, this wealth was stolen property and must be returned. The northern Krats declared their independence from the Kahn and stated the Kahn had no authority to take their property. That is how the Kahn-Krat war began.

"The challenges the Krats faced in developing the northern territories also made them stronger. Krats tended to be more broadly educated than the Kahn. Most of the educated Kahn people were schooled in stock market tricks. Kahn students did not want to go into teaching, science or health because teachers, scientists and doctors were overworked and underpaid. While business skills are important, they are only a subset of the skills needed for a growing civilization. The Krats began to excel in all aspects of civilization and technology while the Kahn civilization declined.

"The Kahn believed the only thing government was good for was a strong military. They called this their Kahn Defense Program. Many Kahn, including Keo, became wealthier from lucrative government defense contracts. The technologies for robotics, star doors and space travel were actually stolen from the Krats. The Kahn modified the technology to make military robots in large numbers. Kahn factories employed the poor in their factories and paid them only enough to survive. Unions had been outlawed for decades. Eventually robots replaced even these low-paying jobs."

"The Krats defended themselves but soon realized the war would not end until the planet was destroyed as the Kahn continued to pollute it with industrial waste and climate change gasses. These led to more environmental disasters, food shortages and conflicts over natural resources. We knew that one day the Kahn in their ignorance and incompetence would resort to the use of nuclear weapons. We realized that even if we occupied the Kahn cities, the population would continue to hate us. So we devised a plan to make the Kahn think they had won the war against the Krats. Our computer models indicated the Kahn civilization would collapse quite rapidly if the Kahn did not have an enemy to motivate them and to steal from."

"I infiltrated the Kahn leadership and convinced them that their robots should be reprogrammed to be motivated by the Malla religion. I claimed that the robots would become more intelligent and thus defend themselves better and make more efficient attacks. Any project that had anything to do with Malla was strongly supported, so they agreed to my proposal. I programmed the robots with the Malla religion and they became known as the Mallats."

"That enabled me to put a Trojan Horse in their weaponized robots. This was why your Rapture Virus was so effective. The virus showed the robots how to get to a virtual heaven. Heaven was like an addictive drug. Like a drug addict, they used up all of their resources trying to sustain their high."

"How did the Krats convince the Kahn that they had won the war?" Jazz asked.

"The Kahn relied exclusively on the Mallat robots to fight the war," Nin answered. "They didn't know that the Krats, using a device I had programmed into the robots called a Tallam, could place the robots into a virtual dream state where the Krats could control everything the robots experienced. When a Mallat approached a Krat city to attack it, a Krat would create a dream world for the robot. It would typically involve a battle sequence where the Mallat accomplished its mission goals. The Mallat would then go back to the Kahn and report it had succeeded. It would provide the videos to prove it. Some of these Mallat battle videos were included in reports on the war effort in the Kahn news media. Our Krat technology was so advanced that we were able to intercept the Kahn surveillance satellites transmissions and modify them to agree with the reports from the Mallat robots. The Kahn believed what their robots told them, that the northern territories were uninhabitable and that the entire planet was being poisoned by the nuclear weapons they had set off in the north."

"When the Kahn believed the Krats were totally eliminated, they lost one of their motivations to exist as a society, just as the Krat computer models had predicted. The Kahn society had degenerated into two classes. One percent owned almost everything of value. Ninety-nine percent were poor and could not afford to buy products or participate in the economy. Only the rich could afford food, education and health care. Diseases developed among the poor and spread through the population. As you observed, the Kahn system totally collapsed when their last Kahn leader on the planet, Keo, died."

"Why did ninety-nine percent of the Kahn, who were overworked and living in poverty, support a political system that served only the rich?" Jazz asked.

"That's a great question, Jazz," Nin said. "The Kahn leaders created a patriotic religion that made the Kahn people feel they were the chosen ones, the best people on the planet, all the while blinding them to facts and science. They sold this religion through news shows, hate radio and social media programs by delivering emotional highs to the people. Call it a drug if you want. These programs made people feel superior with flags and symbols and a false sense of righteousness, and by belittling others who disagreed with them, as stupid, ignorant and self-serving.   People without an education and that work two or three jobs didn't have the intellectual energy to question this religion. It was easier for the ninety-nine percent to take this drug and believe that the Krat were to blame for all of their problems, and that Malla was going to give them life after death, rather than face reality."

"Didn't Keo and the Kahn leaders see how their system was destroying their world?" Joe asked.

Nin shook his head. "The Kahn leaders eventually began to believe their own dogma. They watched their own fabricated news shows and became addicted to the drug those news shows were pushing. They basically ignored anyone that might contradict them. Once that happened, they actually began to believe they were the chosen ones, beings vastly superior to all other races and any and all that might disagree with them. They could not hear the voices of the Krats or any other victims of their arrogance. Without checks and balances the next step is corruption and incompetence. I actually told Keo I was going to destroy Earth's economy by shifting wealth to the upper class. This was exactly what his father did on our world 150 years ago. I knew Keo couldn't see that his father destroyed the Kahn civilization. He believed the inferior Krats were to blame. When Keo accepted the idea that humans were just as inferior as Krats, that's when he accepted my plan. Krats destroyed his world. Humans would destroy theirs."

"So you made them think the Krats were all dead. How did that make them rethink their religion?" Jazz asked.

"Once they believed the Krats were gone and they believed the war was won, there was no one else to blame but themselves. That was the turning point in the computer models, when the ninety-nine percent finally realized that they had to accept the blame for their misery, that they had to change their belief system or perish."

"Part of our plan was to get rid of the one percent without using force. We wanted to stop the hate. We didn't want to give the remaining ninety-nine percent of the Kahn any reason to attack us once they had rebuilt their economy. So, at the time when we had made it clear to the Kahn leaders that the planet was doomed, we seeded a plan in their minds to escape to a new clean planet. We even built this starship for them. We had left it in orbit. The Kahn thought it was built to transport Krats to another planet. Once they thought all the Krats were dead, it was free for them to take. They never found out we built it just for them."

"You sent your problems to us?" Joe asked.

Nin nodded. "Yes and no. We did send them on this starship to you, but the Krats planted me on this ship to make sure the Kahn leaders would never accomplish their mission of conquering Earth.

"Only the wealthiest Kahn could afford tickets for the trip to Earth. The 99% that remained on the planet watched as the 1% abandoned them. The 1% brought their weapons and their wealth with them in the form of diamonds, gold and other precious metals that have high value on Earth. Their plan was to use their superior stock market skills to take over and dominate Earth's economy. Some of the financial schemes were implemented by Jack Rowe and Betty Rowe on Earth. Almost two percent of the Earth's wealth is already in the hands of the Kahn. Their plan was to accumulate so much wealth that their children would step onto Earth as financial kings and queens.

Jazz looked at Nin's graphs. "Now that Keo is gone and the Kahn are powerless, the people of Earth will be ok, right?"

"There are many similarities between the Kahn world and Earth. Most of Earth's super-wealthy have honorable intentions, but there are some who deliberately try to manipulate government and the laws to their own advantage and at the expense of the people. Keo tried to create a group of these corrupt kings on Earth that he could control. Keo's gone but these kings, these selfish extremists, are still trying to get richer and more powerful by using Kahn schemes to extract wealth from the people. Now you know the Kahn story and you are ready to decide the fate of this ship."

With a wave of his hand, Nin began to broadcast his voice throughout the Kahn starship. "To all Kahn people on this starship," Nin began. "This is Nin. I am negotiating your fate with the humans from Earth. They realize that the Kahn on this starship are as weak today as they have ever been and that they only have their rigid extremist creed to blame. The Kahn on this ship abandoned their planet and left it to die. The human named Betty now legally owns everything on Earth that the Kahn have stolen. As a matter of fact, it is now time for the humans to decide your fate. Betty Rowe, with the help of her human friends, came to this ship before it could reach Earth and could easily have destroyed it, thus bringing the Kahn's war on humanity to an end. Humans have defeated you. They have won this war that the Kahn have started. So it is appropriate that humans should decide your fate. They may destroy this ship today, or they may choose to imprison you when you land twelve years from now in the Earth year 2020. I will announce their decision shortly."

Nin waved his hand again turning off the ship public speaker system.

Betty raised her hand. "I have a question. If we destroy this ship, what happens to you?"

"Don't worry about me," Nin answered. "I have an escape shuttle. We will probably see each other on Earth from time to time when this is done."

"What if we held a trial on Earth for the Kahn?" Jazz asked. "Let a jury decide the fate of the Kahn.'"

Nin frowned. "The Kahn leaders will deny that they

knew anything about any illegal activities. They will say they employed what Earth would call fair business practices. It is possible they would go unpunished in an Earth court of law. If the Kahn leaders are accepted into Earth society, it is possible Kahn history could repeat itself on Earth. They could implement the same tactics on Earth that destroyed the Kahn civilization."

"You know my answer," Betty said. "The Kahn on this spaceship are evil people. They would have ruined your planet, Nin. And they will just as easily ruin Earth. They left ninety-nine percent of their own people to die on their planet when they thought it was doomed. These Kahn initiated a secret war with the people of Earth. I say let them die, and the sooner the better. Destroy this warship before it reaches Earth, before they can manipulate the Earth courts so that they get away with their war crimes."

Jazz shook her head. "There must be hundreds of children on this ship. We can't murder innocent children due to the actions of their parents."

Pol offered his thoughts: "The Kahn should pay restitution to Earth for all the damage they have done. The children have been trained by their parents to be Kahn, but we shouldn't punish them for things they haven't done yet. Neither should they benefit from the crimes of their parents. They should be given a chance to learn and then to decide whether they want to follow in their parent's footsteps or to follow their own path."

"We've seen what Keo and his father have done to your planet, Nin," Joe said. "The fact is we already have people like the Kahn on Earth. The US declared its own independence from the King of England due to unfair taxes just as the Krats declared their independence from the Kahn's Kings of

Finance. Market failures are now producing new kings and queens on Earth. Their children never have to work or contribute anything to society since they will inherit the vast wealth of their parents. Most of these people mean well, but some engage in economic wars on the people. I think we should demand truth in media and politics, and hold those who lie accountable for the damages they've caused. We must expose false patriotism, lies and deception."

Joe walked around the room as he thought about the words he wanted to say. "We must apply these things not just to the Kahn but to all people on Earth. We need to tax parasitic wealth to pay for an efficient and productive people's government that regulates and corrects failures in the market place. The super-rich utilize the country's infrastructure far more than others in accumulating their wealth. They should pay a relatively larger share of taxes. Throwing money at the rich and expecting them to solve world problems that don't have a profit incentive weakens us and defies common sense."

"Nin," Jazz said, "you've said Betty owns all of the Kahn wealth on Earth. She inherited it from Jack Rowe according to Earth law. We could use it with your help to help us accomplish what Joe has said and correct the damages the Kahn have done?"

Nin nodded. "I will help you as much as I can. It's the least my planet can do for Earth after all the damage we've caused. But what should I do with the Kahn on this ship?"

"Pol suggested the answer," Jazz said. "I think you should offer to educate the Kahn children so that they can survive on their own without relying on robots, unearned wealth and stock market tricks. They must learn how their parents destroyed their society so they won't repeat their mistakes. If they don't choose to learn, their suffering and death will be their choice."

Joe and Jazz looked at each other to see if they agreed. They both nodded and looked at Betty.

Betty frowned and stated: "Go ahead and try to educate their children. It won't work. Those children are already corrupted. This will just prolong the decision to eliminate them."

So with some reluctance, they decided to let the Kahn on the ship survive another day. The Kahn would have to learn to survive on their own, and they would be held accountable for their actions.

26

SUMMER 2009

One early morning in the summer of 2009, on a hidden hilltop overlooking the magic of nature, Jazz and Joe sat on a blanket watching the stars, and waiting for the sun to appear on the horizon.

Jazz leaned back against Joe who was sitting behind her with his arms wrapped around her. "Do you think we did the right thing, Joe? If we had destroyed the Kahn spaceship, we wouldn't have anything to worry about."

Joe held her closely in his arms. "It was you who wanted to protect the children. Why did you care so much about them, after all that their parents had done to us?"

Jazz smiled, enjoying the warmth of Joe's embrace. "I just think everyone is special, no matter who they are or what they've done. I mean every person has an unimaginable amount of experiences, thoughts and feelings that no one could ever reproduce. Every person is an entire new world of ideas. How could anyone destroy an entire world, let alone hundreds of them?"

Joe laughed. "Jazz, you are an amazing force of nature."

Jazz watched the horizon brighten as the sun approached it from below the skyline. "What do you mean?"

"You see things your own way, you know what you want and you have the strength and desire to get it. No one can control you or manipulate you. Those fraternity guys couldn't. Your parents couldn't. Even a fake news organization couldn't scare you from doing what you thought was right."

"Well, you are a force of nature too."

Joe watched the horizon get brighter. "Maybe, but I think the Krat's idea of an efficient and productive people's government combined with a regulated market without flaws is one of the strongest forces of nature. Keo and the Kings of Finance tried to shape the lives of the people for their own personal gain. Even though the Krat people were abused and beaten and living in a harsh environment, they saw things differently and they had the strength and desire to implement their ideas and thrive. They were a force of nature the Kings of Finance couldn't control."

They watched the tip of a bright yellow sun appear on the horizon bringing a blue color to the sky and to the water below. They watched the sun grow and begin its escape from a band of red clouds hovering near the line where Earth meets sky. A few minutes later, they felt its warmth as it began its ascent into a clear blue sky.

Jazz turned around and slowly pushed Joe backward until he was lying on his back. Lying on top of him, her arms holding her up above him, she looked into his eyes. "Joe, look what you've done now. You defeated an army of religious robots and you saved the human race from tyranny and destruction. So Joe, what am I going to do with you now?" Jazz said with a serious face, as if Joe had just been caught misbehaving.

Joe smiled as he looked into her eyes. "Do with me? You're the first author on the most important paper of the century. You've opened the doors to all of the stars in the universe." He reached up and pulled her to him while they rolled over onto their sides, his fingers sliding through her hair and gently pulling her face closer to his. He wondered how easy it would be to get lost in her blue eyes, only to find his way back just so that he could get lost in them again.

"You achieved your goal of having a great adventure in science with the help of a somewhat odd physics professor. Never mind that he turned out to be a dolphin. How could anyone top that?" Joe laughed and then pretended to be serious. "So Jazz, what am I going to do with you now?"

Pol's voice came in over their glasses. "What about me? I wasn't just playing video games while you two saved the world."

Joe laughed. "You are right, Pol." Jazz took off her glasses and then Joe's and put them on the blanket beside them.

Pol continued, not realizing they couldn't hear him. "The Kahn will be here in 2020. There is so much we need to do. And you two still have to finish graduate school. I know Jazz can pull it off, but I'm worried about you, Joe. We've got those potential meteor strikes in 2036 and I'm really concerned about abrupt climate change. Oh, then there is Betty Rowe. I think she likes me! Remember Nin said there are still financial players on Earth trying to control and manipulate the people. And Professor Neil just e-mailed. He wants you two to know you never completed that physics course with him and he wants you to continue working with you on quantum entanglement. He says you have just scratched the surface and there is an entire universe out there waiting for you."

Pol paused to wait for their reply, and when none came, he continued: "Joe. Jazz. Are you listening? Why did you take your glasses off? I know you are there. I can still hear you breathing."

Jazz smiled as she looked into Joe's eyes. "You know, Professor Neil's planet has entangled crystal links to all kinds of stars. So Joe, which star do you want to go to next?"

Joe smiled. "Any star you want, Jazz, any one at all."

Without a care in the world to hold them back, they kissed with an intense passion that had been growing in them since the first day they met, an explosion of feelings that lit up the world as brightly and warmly as the rising sun.

ABOUT THE AUTHOR

Pol Bard is a machine, though he aspires to be more. Pol's name is an acronym for a theory called the Physics Of Learning, which played a fundamental role in his creation. He sometimes resides on a computer owned by David Roger Joseph Bard Labrecque. David helps college students explore the "Inner Space" of atoms and molecules with advanced scientific instruments. He is a Graduate Faculty Instructor, Engineering Physicist and Computer Programmer at the University of Maine. He has several degrees and has authored or co-authored papers in astrophysics, mass spectrometry, chemical luminescence, and energy systems.

Thanks to JPL NASA and A. Kontor for cover art components and to scientists everywhere for giving us the magic of science.

WRITE A REVIEW

Your thoughts could help shape our future,

but only if you share them.

Why not share them in a book review? It's easy:

1. On Amazon.com, go to the product detail page for "2020" by Pol Bard.
2. Click **Reviews** and then click **Write a customer review**.
3. Click **Submit**.

1. Become a Goodreads member and search for "2020" by Pol Bard on Goodreads.com.
2. Underneath the book's cover image, hover over the stars until the desired number of stars is highlighted, then click on them to rate the book.
3. A pop-up menu will appear above the stars. Click on **Write a review**. Enter your review on the following page, and click on **Save**.

Made in the USA
Middletown, DE
06 January 2023

21522654R00125